Turn Left
On
Green

Turn Left
On
Green

A Novel of
Stock Car
Racing

By Clyde Bolton

RIVER CITY PUBLISHING
Montgomery, Alabama

Printed in the United States.
First Edition

Library of Congress Cataloging-in-Publication Data:
Bolton, Clyde.
Turn left on green : a novel of stock car racing / by Clyde Bolton.
p. cm.
ISBN 1-57966-027-4 (alk. paper)
1. Automobile racing drivers--Fiction. 2. Women sportswriters--Fiction. 3. Stock car racing--Fiction. I. Title.
PS3552.O5877 T87 2002
813'.54--dc21
2002000226

To Bobby and Judy Allison

Thanks to all the men and women of NASCAR—
in the offices, in the race cars, in the garages.
Your years of friendship contributed mightily to this book.

Chapter 1

Miss Barrett," the copy boy said, "Mr. Watkins wants to see you in his office."

Beth Barrett sighed, closed her eyes, and nodded. "Thanks," she said, brushing the back of her hand across the blonde bangs of her Dutch boy haircut. It had been one of those days: the coach she had been assigned to interview had forgotten their appointment and gone golfing instead; an advertising salesman had scraped the fender of her sports car in the parking lot; the new telephone system somehow had become crossed up, so that subscribers' complaints intended for the circulation department were coming to her desk.

And now, just as she had gotten her thoughts focused on the story she was writing, Blake Watkins, sports editor of *The Birmingham News*, was summoning her. But one didn't keep Watkins waiting, so she straightened her skirt and walked across the room to his office. He glanced up, saw her through the wide plate glass window, and motioned for her to enter.

"How's it going, Beth?" Watkins said, offering a seat in front of his cluttered desk.

"Fine," she said. "You?"

Blake Watkins was informal, friendly, rumpled—an ideal boss, as long as his orders were carried out, his wishes obeyed to the letter. He liked Beth, admired her *chittlin's*, as he put it in the vernacular of his rural upbringing, because she wanted to be a sports writer, an ambition frowned upon by some of the male members of the newspaper's sports staff. Four years before, just three days out of college, Beth had interviewed for the job, eagerly spreading her clippings from the University of Alabama newspaper before Watkins, forcing herself to look straight into his amused eyes—and the sports editor had hired her that very afternoon.

"I want to make a change or two in the sports department," Watkins said now, looking at her through the frame of his two unshined loafers that he swung onto his desk as he reared back in a scarred swivel chair.

"Have I done something wrong?" Beth asked.

"Nope," Watkins assured her. "It's even a promotion of sorts for you, though the money will be the same. I'm going to take you off the small-college beat and put you on stock car racing."

"But racing is Charlie Murphy's beat," she said. "Why does he want to give it up?"

"I doubt that he will want to," Watkins said. "I haven't told him yet."

Beth knew Charlie Murphy didn't like her. He considered her a female interloper in what should be an exclusively male province. He cracked remarks about the imagined sexual preferences of women athletes and women sports writers, and made sure they got back to her. A good-morning nod was the extent of his friendliness toward her.

The guys on the *News* kidded Charlie Murphy that the first race he covered for the paper was run on the day the second automobile was built. He thrived on the camaraderie of the drivers, mechanics, and car owners and guarded his beat zealously. He wouldn't even take a vacation in the summer because he didn't want a young general assignment man substituting for two weeks.

Beth had no stomach for replacing him as the racing writer.

"Charlie has covered racing for, what, twenty years?" she said. "I love his stuff." She lowered her eyes, a sure sign she was lying, one she feared Watkins recognized.

"Twenty-six years—exactly your age," Watkins said. "That's the whole problem. His stuff is stale. If I have to read another Rusty Wallace profile by Charlie Murphy I'll jump out the window."

"Why me?" Beth asked.

"Racing's a vibrant, colorful sport. You're a vibrant, colorful writer who'll produce some fresh copy. Besides, didn't you used to date David Marlow? You must know something about it."

"How did you know that?"

"Well, you didn't intend it to be a deep, dark secret, did you? It's an interesting little item of office gossip, I'd say."

"I was a freshman in college." Beth said. "David was driving on the short tracks in Alabama then, trying to get a break. There was a circuit of speedways, and on Friday nights he ran at a little dirt track near Tuscaloosa. Just as a lark, some of us college girls went to the races one night. After they were over, the fans could go down into the pits and look at the cars and meet the drivers. David won that night, we struck up a conversation, and we dated a few times. But within a few weeks he got a chance to drive a better car for an owner in Virginia, and I didn't see him anymore. That hardly qualifies me as an expert on racing."

"Well, David Marlow doesn't have to drive on dirt tracks now," Watkins said. "He's a bona fide star of Winston Cup stock car racing on the high-banked superspeedways. I was glancing through a guide on Charlie's desk earlier today and noticed he has been runner-up for the championship the last two seasons, and he earned nearly five million dollars each of those years."

Beth's thoughts traveled backward seven years. She remembered how David had looked the first night she had seen him. Except for the white figure-8 protected by his goggles, his face, neck, and helmet had been covered with red clay. She had laughed at the sight and impetuously opened her compact and held the mirror in front of him. "Really, you have too much makeup on," she said.

David Marlow immediately took his revenge, turning the joke around by taking the stranger in his muddy arms and kissing her on the lips, to the delight of her companions and the other spectators. "Now I've shared it with you," he said.

She was embarrassed, but she forced herself to be a good sport about it since she had started the whole thing. "You drove a fine race," she said, smiling. "Congratulations." She supposed he had driven a fine race. He had won. That was the object, wasn't it?

She was glad when her friends didn't want to go to the track with her the next Friday. She went alone, and soon she and David were dating. He could only afford to take her to the movies and for a hamburger afterward. He worked all day at his job at an auto parts store, half the night on his race car, and every spare cent went into improving the bat- tered but fast machine. He was ambitious, determined to make it to the big league Winston Cup circuit. She had never doubted that he would.

She remembered the nights when they had stood outside her dormi- tory, David kissing her goodnight, neither wanting the kiss to end. She might have fallen in love with David Marlow and, she believed, he with her, had the opportunity to drive on the Virginia circuit not come along. David moved hundreds of miles away and they hadn't seen each other since.

"How much does the driver get?" Watkins said, interrupting her brief reverie.

"What?"

"How much of that almost five million dollars did Marlow get? Surely not all of it. A lot of people are involved in a racing team."

"I have no idea," Beth said.

"Charlie knows," Watkins said, wagging his forefinger, "but he no doubt figures that's such a basic fact of racing that everybody else knows, too, so he doesn't tell his readers. That's what I mean, Beth: you'll give us fresh stories because you'll be fresh."

She didn't want to kindle the open enmity of Charlie Murphy. And, she forced herself to admit silently, she wasn't comfortable with the prospect of renewing her acquaintance with David Marlow. People change in seven years. If he had changed as much inwardly as his circumstances had changed, he would be like a different person. Besides, he probably had married, and covering an old boyfriend who was hitched to another woman would be awkward.

"I'd rather not move to stock car racing," she said sheepishly.

Watkins frowned and took a deep breath. She knew what was coming. "I wasn't asking your *druthers*," he said. "That's the way it will be. I'll tell Charlie, and you can get with him and find out just how . . ." The sports editor craned his neck and saw Charlie Murphy stepping off the elevator into the newsroom. Their eyes met and he motioned to Murphy to come to his office.

Murphy flopped into a chair without being invited to sit, loosened his tie, and undid the button at the neck of his sweat-soiled shirt. "How're you, Blake?" he asked, not even acknowledging Beth's presence.

"Okay," Watkins said. "Charlie, I was wondering—don't you ever get tired of covering racing?"

Murphy was a dumpy, baldheaded man with a perennially flushed face, a condition exacerbated by, so office gossip told it, regular nips from a flask in a bathroom stall. He was fifty-three, five years older than Blake Watkins. He never seemed particularly happy or particularly sad, and the emotion in his voice when he answered the sports editor was boredom: "Racing's the *only* sport. You miss a bunt, you lose a ball game; you miss a turn, you lose your life. How can you get tired of covering something with those stakes?"

"Charlie, I'm going to take you off racing and put you on the Birmingham Barons baseball team," Watkins said.

"What!" Murphy blurted. "I've covered racing for the *News* since you were a cub, Blake. Hell, I was the first full-time racing writer the paper ever had."

"I know that, Charlie," the sports editor said, "and I'm grateful for all you've done to build up our racing coverage, and the paper is grateful; but we want a fresh slant on racing. And Strunk has been on baseball seven seasons, so we can use the fresh slant on baseball that you'll give us, too."

"Baseball? God, Blake, I couldn't stay awake through three innings of a baseball game if I had to. And Ray Strunk doesn't know a race car from a taxi. It's a mistake."

Watkins's short fuse was burned out. "You're the baseball writer, starting with tomorrow's game against Chattanooga, Mr. Murphy," he said icily. "Get Strunk to take you out to the ballpark tonight and introduce you to the players."

Murphy's eyes were narrow slits. "And I suppose you want me to take him to a race track and introduce him to the *players*," he said acidly.

"I didn't say Strunk was going on the racing beat," Watkins growled. "He's going to golf, that new kid who's on golf is going to the small colleges, and Beth is going to racing."

Charlie Murphy bellowed a sarcastic, cruel laugh. "You're putting this girl on the racing beat? Damn, Blake, have you lost your mind?"

Watkins leaped to his feet. "No, but you might lose your *job*. I don't give a damn if you've worked here a hundred years, you'd better believe I'm your boss."

Murphy's lips quivered and now the anger in his eyes was directed toward Beth. She glanced at the floor, as if avoiding two malevolent rays that would somehow diminish her if she met them with her eyes. He turned and started out the office door.

"Charlie," Watkins said, stopping him. "How much of his official earnings would David Marlow keep?"

"A top driver like Marlow would get half, plus a good salary," Murphy said, prudence now vying with anger in his voice. "Everybody knows that."

"No," Watkins said with the satisfaction of a man who has proved his point, "everybody doesn't know that."

BETH DROVE HER red Mazda Miata sports car through the Appalachian foothills, heading east from Birmingham, and though she knew her cheeks and nose were reddening, she left the little convertible's top down.

She remembered when David's old Ford had broken down on just such a nippy fall day. It was a machine that had lived for more than two hundred thousand miles, thanks to the mechanical expertise of David and his friends, but as she and David headed toward a picnic it suffered a terminal stroke, expiring with an explosion under the hood that left engine parts in a stream of oil on the highway. It was the car with which David towed his racer, and the back seat was grease-coated because there reposed his tools.

She remembered how embarrassed he was and how he told her he didn't know what he would do, because he couldn't race without a tow car, but he had no money to buy one. But, through it all, he had been concerned because her outing was spoiled, because she was disappointed, because instead of spreading a picnic lunch on a blanket beside Lake Logan Martin, they were sitting at a concrete picnic table at a rest stop a quarter mile down the road from the corpse of the car.

Knowing David had taught her a lesson that later had guided her judgment at the newspaper: that preconceived notions of what a person must be like—because he was in a certain vocation, avocation, or circumstances—often were mistaken.

She and her friends had first visited the little dirt track with the attitude of merrymakers going to watch the monkeys at the zoo. She half expected the drivers to hoist a jug of moonshine before climbing into their cars to attempt vehicular homicide. But in David she met a man who was a hard competitor but who never crowded another driver beyond accepted limits; who could enjoy the sports page but who avidly read Faulkner and Wolfe; who could afford only movies but who selected good ones; who could hold his gaze on his goal despite privation but who could sympathize with Beth, who was eight years younger, because she was a freshman away from home for the first time in her life.

Was he still the same principled, sensitive, alive man, or had the cost of success, or success itself, blunted his feelings? She thought of the song in which a star said there had been a load of compromising on the road to his horizon. Had David compromised and left some of himself at the bargaining table? Or was the man behind the wheel at the glamorous tracks the same one who had been covered with the red clay of the bullrings?

Bethany Bridget Barrett was wondering about David when she almost missed her exit off the interstate. She braked sharply and turned without a signal. A sputtering driver behind her made a crude gesture as he passed.

Beth sped five miles on the four-lane road, and then she saw it. She stopped her car on the shoulder and stared at Talladega Superspeedway, named for a nearby town that was the track's mailing address.

The track was awesome. She remembered that a colleague had told her it would hold thirty-two stadiums the size of the Rose Bowl. She had seen it before, of course, but now that it was to become part of her job, of her life, it was even more stunning, even more impressive. She gawked unashamedly at the 2.66-mile speedway before her.

Beth picked up her credentials at the press office, flashed them to the security guard at the gate, and drove through the tunnel that bored underneath the track's fourth turn. Inside, she marveled at the five-story-high turns that were banked at thirty-three degrees. She heard the growl of a race car that was approaching the backstretch. It zoomed by her at a speed she had heretofore seen only in the sky, the number on its top visible as the car clung to the bank of the turn.

It was Thursday, the first day of practice, the day before qualifying runs for Sunday's five-hundred-miler began. Beth gazed at the frontstretch grandstand that stretched for nearly a mile and tried to imagine the speedway as it would be Sunday, with nearly two hundred thousand fans in the stands and infield, and forty-three cars dueling inches apart. It must be awesome. No wonder Charlie Murphy had loved racing and guarded his beat.

"Go to the garage and introduce yourself to the drivers," a *Birmingham News* desk man who had covered racing for another paper had advised her. "Tell them you're new at this and ask for their help. Most of them are nice guys." She parked her car in the media lot beside the garage, waved her credentials at a second security guard, and walked toward the long concrete building.

Inside, cars were on jackstands, mechanics' legs sticking out from under them as they adjusted the chassis for the particular characteristics of the NASCAR circuit's biggest track. Other mechanics were buried under hoods, tuning engines, and one young gofer cackled when a mechanic startled Beth by revving his motor.

She ignored a soft whistle as she sauntered past the garage spaces, studying the cars, which were brightly painted with every color under the sun, each bearing the advertising message of its sponsor on the rear fenders. She felt several sets of eyes on her designer jeans as she proceeded.

"They're barbarians, let out of their cages on Thursday mornings, reincarcerated on Sunday nights," a voice said.

Beth turned to see a tall, straight man with thick iron-gray hair, about fifty, his white shirt three-buttons open, two obviously expensive gold chains hanging in the gray hair of his chest. He wore jeans and short boots that she recognized as custom made. "My name is Herman Lanston," he said. "I don't believe I've ever seen you in a garage before."

"I'm Beth Barrett," she said, extending her hand. "I'm the new racing writer for *The Birmingham News*. This is my first race."

"This may be my millionth race," Herman Lanston said pleasantly. "I hope you will enjoy the sport as much as I have. That car in the end space, the blue Chevrolet, is mine. Vern Parchman is my driver."

"Vern Parchman? He's the champion. He won eight races and earned nearly seven million dollars last year," Beth said.

"Perhaps this is your first race, but you've done your homework, Miss . . . may I call you Beth? I would be pleased to introduce you to Vern and to anyone else you care to meet, or to help you become acquainted with racing in any way that I might. Racing is an arcane sport. We grow up knowing about football and baseball because we're constantly exposed to it in school, but we aren't necessarily exposed to racing."

The man had a nice style. He was charming. "Thank you. I'd like that," Beth said.

Vern Parchman was sitting on a workbench, playing hearts with another driver, while six mechanics danced about his car, which bore the words *Lanston Farms* in foot-high white letters on the rear fender. "Vern, would you come over here a second?" Herman Lanston yelled over the roar of a motor.

Parchman followed Beth and Lanston to a splotch of sunshine outside the garage. "This is Vern Parchman," Lanston said. "This is Beth Barrett of *The Birmingham News*."

Parchman was as old as the car owner. She had read that he was a crafty veteran who rarely led in the first four hundred miles of a five-hundred-mile race. He preferred to let the hard chargers wear their cars out while he conserved his energy and his racer. Then, at the end, he had only two or three contenders to battle.

"Hello," he said.

"How do you feel about Sunday's race?" Beth asked.

Parchman shrugged his shoulders. "It's just another race. I've got as good a chance as anybody, better than most, like always."

He didn't smile and there was no warmth in his voice. Beth could guess how Vern Parchman felt about women sports writers.

"Come on, or Vern will talk your ear off," Herman Lanston said, chuckling and placing his hand lightly on her shoulder for direction.

"Where is David Marlow's car?" Beth asked.

"Marlow? I doubt that they're here yet. They'll probably arrive later today. They ran tests here last week, so their car should already be dialed in to the track."

"Dialed in?"

"That's a racing term. Each speedway is different. Daytona's two and a half miles. Atlanta's a mile and a half. Dover's a mile. Bristol's a half mile. And their shapes and degree of banking are different. Sonoma and Watkins Glen are road courses. We run a thirty-six-race schedule on twenty-three tracks, and a car has to be dialed in to handle on each track. That requires different chassis setups. In fact, a given speedway may change between its first and second race of the season, one of which may be run in cold weather, the other under a boiling sun."

"I've got a lot to learn," Beth said.

"Newspapers interest the public in racing, the public becomes acquainted with Lanston Farms through seeing the name on my car, Lanston Farms sells more canned goods, I make more money," Lanston said. "Helping you learn is the least I can do."

Chapter 2

Beth sat in the bucket seat of the race car, surrounded by roll bars. She felt as if she were in an army tank, bulletproof to all harm. Then she pressed the accelerator and the unmuffled motor assaulted her ears and shook her body. Now she felt as if she were inside a space-ship.

The sensations of the sport—yes! She realized instantly how men—and women— became captives of stock car racing, how their lives became centered on the endless left turn on green.

Herman Lanston had introduced her to seven more drivers, all of whom were cordial. One had helped her through the window of his car, let her sit in the seat, even let her goose the accelerator.

"How about that?" the driver said, placing his hands on her waist and effortlessly lifting her five-foot, two-inch, 109-pound body from its awkward position as she exited the car.

Lanston took over. "Let's go to my motor home and have a cold lemonade and a salmon salad before the action really begins," he said. Beth had eaten only a piece of toast before beginning the forty-mile drive from Birmingham to the speedway. Food would be welcome.

Lanston's motor home was a marvelous machine parked outside the garage area. Its blue paint matched that of his race car. He opened the door to an interior of leather upholstery and rosewood paneling and tables. "This is beautiful," Beth said. "It's a rolling palace."

"Just a humble little home away from home," Lanston said, chuckling. "No, Lanston Farms has done well. I like fine things, and I buy them if I can, and if they aren't fine enough I improve on them. I had the original interior torn out and replaced with this. My only regret is that my wife isn't here to share it with me. She loved racing, the trips, the people. I'm a widower."

He opened the refrigerator and inventoried its contents. "Champagne? Beer? Wine? You name it."

"Lemonade is fine," Beth said.

The pleasant October morning had been overruled by the midday sun, and no breeze was stirring in the bowl of the speedway. Beth was comfortable in the air-conditioned motor home, but she also was anxious to get to work on her new beat, to interview a driver. Then a realization struck her: if Charlie Murphy had ever written a feature on a car owner, she had never read it. She would interview Herman Lanston. After all, Blake Watkins wanted a fresh slant on racing.

"No, please," Lanston said, raising his open right hand when she proposed the story. "My satisfaction comes from seeing my car in Victory Lane. I do nothing to put it there except supply the raw material— commonly known as money. The crew builds the racer, Vern Parchman's skill sends it to the head of the pack. I appreciate the thought very much, but I'd rather not."

She was disappointed, but she was impressed. Few persons on this earth would say no to a complimentary newspaper feature. One couldn't fault genuine modesty.

"The lemonade and salad were delicious," Beth said, smiling at the handsome man who nodded a *you're welcome* across the table from her. "And I appreciate your taking up time with a racing rookie."

"You have made my morning most pleasant," Lanston said, holding open the door of the motor home.

Beth stepped from the lavish vehicle, Lanston at her heels, and as she did she saw a huge tractor-trailer enter the garage compound. It was followed by a silver Mercury with David Marlow at the wheel.

David glanced toward Lanston's motor home, fifty yards away. His eyes fastened on Beth. He watched for a moment, then turned his head back toward the rear of the truck, obviously having decided it couldn't be her.

"There's your Mr. Marlow," Lanston said. "The man who makes our Victory Lane champagne taste perfect."

Beth looked at Lanston. The pleasant expression she had grown accustomed to seeing had turned into a smirk. His eyes narrowed as he watched the truck stop in front of the garage, David's car beside it.

"David has been second to Parchman in the championship points standings the last two years, hasn't he?" she said, curious at the change in the man, prodding him to say more.

"There is no such thing as second in anything," Lanston said. "In a forty-three-car race there is a winner and there are forty-two losers. In the points standings there are a champion and a lot of losers. Vern is the champion, Marlow one of the losers."

"But you said he is the man who makes your champagne taste perfect," Beth reminded. "You must consider him something special."

Lanston realized he was being picked by a reporter, albeit a pretty one, and the smile returned to his face. "Just about every one of the drivers is a great competitor," he said noncommittally. "It's a great sport."

"Again, thanks for the introductions, the lemonade, and the salad," Beth said. "I think I'll stroll through the garage."

"The door will be unlocked," he said. "The refrigerator's stocked. Help yourself anytime."

The glimpse of David kindled Beth's desire to see him, to learn of his life these last seven years. Without difficulty, she put her misgivings about renewing their acquaintance behind her.

Beth walked across the asphalt expanse toward David's space in the garage. She saw that his crew was unloading the race car from the truck, though, and she decided not to interrupt. She wanted David's full attention.

She wandered down the line of cars that faced David's line. They were separated by a workbench that ran the length of the garage; it held large tool chests, fans, and coolers packed with soft drinks. No one from David's side was paying her any attention.

She mused about the turns life can take. She was born into a comfortable Montgomery family, her father a dentist, her mother a college history professor. Their only other child was a boy who received a football scholarship to the University of Alabama.

Their country club membership had meant cotillions and receptions to her mother, golf to her father and brother. Despite her mother's efforts to mold her to the social graces, she had followed the men on to the course. Her mother shook her head when Beth's father bought his blonde girl a miniature set of clubs.

She was a tomboy at first, begging to go fishing, playing in the tree houses of the neighborhood boys. But she grew to high school age and the tomboy was replaced by a "good sport" whose clean, ruddy good looks—never requiring makeup—weren't lost on the boys. They liked the slight girl with the Dutch boy haircut and the good humor, liked her for a date or for a friend. She opened males' eyes whether she wore jeans at cheerleading practice or a gown at the junior-senior prom. It was not surprising that she was a runaway selection as Senior Sweetheart, a designation that somewhat appeased her mother.

Influenced by her brother, she attended the University of Alabama, again distressing her mother by majoring in journalism and playing on the women's golf team. The only job open on the college newspaper was for a sports writer, and she eagerly grabbed it. She was sports editor her senior year.

Less than two weeks after she wrote her final story for the school paper, she was on the sports staff of *The Birmingham News*, the largest paper in the state. Now, without benefit of ever having seen a major race, she was about to cover a five-hundred-miler, one of the events on the National Association for Stock Car Auto Racing's Winston Cup schedule. That was a long way from the spring cotillion.

Beth glanced between cases of spark plugs on the workbench toward David's garage space. The crew had unloaded the race car, and David stood alone, removing his helmet from a cloth bag. She stepped around the workbench and walked up behind him.

"Wipe the red clay off your face, buddy," she said.

David turned slowly, a smile already on his face before his eyes met hers. "Go stick your finger back in the dike, Dutch boy," he said.

They embraced, and she was momentarily miffed with herself because tears of joy rushed to her eyes. *My gosh, I'm supposed to be a professional, a sports writer.*

He kissed her on the lips, not a kiss of casual greeting but a lingering welcome back into his life. She knew she was blushing as crewmen at the next car laughed and choroused, "Awright!"

"I saw you when I drove in," David said, releasing her, "but I decided I must be mistaken. I couldn't imagine what in the world you would be doing in the garage area of the biggest speedway on the planet, so I decided it was somebody else."

"I used to frequent the smallest speedway on the planet," she said.

"Gosh, that was a long time ago," David said. "It seems like that was another world."

Despite his obvious pleasure at seeing her, the words disappointed her. Perhaps he was saying she was from a long time ago—from a life that no longer existed.

"I'm a sports writer for *The Birmingham News*," she said. "Racing is my new beat. This is my first race."

"You really went through with it," he stated more than asked. "You said you wanted to be a sports writer, but I thought you'd change your mind."

"You've become quite a success since you were a dirt dauber," Beth said.

"Dirt dauber," David whispered, savoring the words. "When have I heard that expression? That's what they called us when we were slinging that Alabama clay all over each other and the fans, too."

She stared at him until he was embarrassed. Maturity had made a pleasing package intriguing. He was six feet tall with black hair and dark eyes, the genetic gifts of a Spanish grandmother. An inch-long scar on his right cheek—she suspected from a racing accident—enhanced the picture rather than detracted from it. He wore a white polo shirt, white slacks, matching shoes, and a baby blue sport coat, the light clothes accentuating the midnight coloring of the man. Beth knew that, at thirty-four, David Marlow must be the star of many a female racing fan's fantasies.

"Well," he said finally, "since you're a rookie at this, I'll introduce you around, help you any way I can."

"Thanks, David," Beth said. "Mr. Lanston introduced me to most of the few drivers who have arrived. But I'm sure I'll be asking you a million questions."

"Yeah, I noticed you were with Moneybags," he said. "Beauty and the beast."

She looked for a sign he was joking but found none. "He seems nice enough," she said. "Hey, talk about moneybags, the NASCAR record book says you can afford better than an old Ford with two hundred thousand miles on the speedometer these days."

She was surprised that he wasn't amused. "Well, there's money and then there's money. Lanston could buy this speedway and forget the next day he'd bought it."

She had prodded Lanston about David, but she didn't want to prod David. "Bring me up to date from that day you said adios and hied off to Virginia on the road to fame and fortune," she said.

"Let's sit in my car," he suggested. "It's hot out here." He opened the door of his passenger car, a big Mercury Grand Marquis, for her, and Beth sank into the rich leather seat.

He flicked on the air conditioner and stared straight ahead as his crew began to prep his white Ford race car. "I told you when I left for Virginia that the ride I was accepting would be only one step away from the big league," he began. "Well, it was.

"The owner of that team had a lot of money, at least for that level of racing, and he didn't mind spending it on the car. He had had a couple of older, cautious drivers. He wanted a young fellow who would mash the accelerator, and you weren't in trouble with him if he had to take the car home in a basket.

"We won a lot of short-track races that season, but the one that really counted was here at this speedway. It was a Saturday preliminary in the Busch Grand National series before the Sunday Winston Cup race. In addition to our regular Friday night and Saturday night bullring outings, the owner financed five Grand National races, all on superspeedways, and one was at Talladega. I passed a faster car on the last lap to win, and all the Winston Cup folks saw it.

"It's tough to get a top car in Winston Cup. The things cost a fortune, and nobody wants to hand one over to a rookie with no Cup experience. 'You can't get a ride until you get experience, and you can't get experience until you get a ride,' the old saying goes. So even though my winning the Saturday race here had to impress them, none of the big-buck teams made me an offer.

"But a Midwesterner who sold pre-fab houses and backed his own Winston Cup racing team did. His wasn't one of the better cars because the money just wasn't there, but I drove it to its limits, and our positions were usually better than the car should have finished. I even ran fifth a couple of times, beating some of the rich teams.

"Lanston was impressed and he offered me his car. I drove for him a season and a half and . . ."

"You drove for Herman Lanston?" Beth interrupted. "I didn't know that."

"We won ten races in a season and a half, and I was established,"

David said. "The next year I joined my present team, Bibley Designs, and I've been its driver ever since."

Beth's journalistic curiosity overruled her good manners. "There's a half-season missing," she said.

"After I left Lanston I fished the rest of the season," he said. "A friend in Florida has a big boat."

She was dying to know why David and Herman Lanston would break up in the middle of the racing season, but she wouldn't ask. There was one question that couldn't be put off any longer, though.

"Is there a Mrs. Marlow?"

"No. I'm still a bachelor. This can be a cruel sport. I've seen what can happen to the families of drivers."

Her silence told him she didn't know what he was talking about. "Beth, my brother Pete was killed in a race a few years ago," he said.

She was stunned. "Little Pete? The boy who used to help you with your car when he was, what, in junior high? Oh, David, I'm sorry. I didn't know."

"He was a rookie, just twenty years old. He was driving in his first Winston Cup race. It was news for a day, then it was forgotten."

He was obviously uncomfortable with the subject so she asked, "Where's home, David?"

"Daytona Beach. Living there means I have to do a lot of traveling that wouldn't be necessary if I were in a more central location, like Charlotte, but it's worth it to me to be on the ocean. The Atlantic laps right up to the seawall at my house. And, of course, a couple of Winston Cup races a year are run at Daytona Beach."

"I love the ocean, too," Beth said.

"The beach there is flat and hard, and I jog six miles on it every day when I'm home. A race driver is just as much an athlete as a baseball player. You don't just hop into a car and drive five hundred miles at Darlington, South Carolina, in early September unless you're physically prepared."

A man in an immaculate white uniform tapped on the windshield of

David's car, and he rolled down the window. "She's ready when you are," the man said.

"I've got to make some practice laps," David told Beth, reaching across her lap to open the door. "I want you to meet this fellow."

The mechanic smiled admiringly at the girl with the sunburned nose. He was short and wiry, no more than five and a half feet, and, she reckoned, maybe seventy years old, though his black hair was still fighting a valiant battle against the white. "Beth Barrett, Pappy Draper," said David. "Pappy's my crew chief, father confessor, and chili chef. Beth's an old friend who covers racing for *The Birmingham News*."

"Pleased to meet you," Pappy Draper said. "Why don't you climb up on top of our truck with me and watch David run?"

"I'd love it," Beth said, and Pappy motioned her to the tractor-trailer rig. They climbed the steel ladder that was bolted onto the side. From the top they watched David disappear into the race car hauler, as other crewmen pushed the car from the garage into the sunshine that warmed the October day.

A breeze was pleasant against her sunburn. In the distance she could see Mount Cheaha, the highest point in Alabama. "Great view," Pappy said—looking only at her.

"I'll bet you're a piece of work," Beth said, grinning. She liked the little man.

"I'm harmless," he said. "Totally devoted to putting David into Victory Lane. He's good folks—the best. If he likes *you*, you have to be good folks, too."

"I knew him when he was driving on the dirt tracks," Beth said. "That was a long time ago."

Pappy pointed, and Beth saw David exiting the car hauler. He had changed into a flameproof uniform and he carried his helmet under his arm. His black hair contrasted with the white driver's suit, and she could see the darkness of his eyes as he smiled and waved.

David effortlessly climbed through the window of the race car, and the unmuffled machine came to life with a blast of noise that caused Beth to cover her ears. He eased the car onto the track and drove two laps on the flat apron, allowing the motor to warm up. Then she saw the car pick up speed and climb onto the steep banking of the first turn, and when it passed before them thirty seconds later it was a missile.

Pappy Draper reached for the stopwatch that hung on a shoelace around his neck, sighted the car against a broadcast tower, and pressed a button. "All right!" he exclaimed when David completed a lap. He pulled a printed conversion table from his shirt pocket, found the speed beside the time David had recorded, and said, "He did 190.279 right out of the box! How do you like that?"

"That's super," Beth said. She guessed it must be.

"This is the best car we've ever brought to Talladega," Pappy told her. "It's gonna take a monster to beat us Sunday. We'll win the pole tomorrow."

He reset the stopwatch, and in less than a minute he yelled again, "An airplane! That thing's an airplane!" He pointed to 191.004 on the conversion table.

David returned to the garage area, cutting the engine and letting the car coast into its space under the roof. He was smiling when his feet hit the ground and he removed his helmet.

Pappy Draper scurried down the ladder with an enthusiasm that belied his age, Beth behind him. He ran to the car, eager to hear David's appraisal. His smile widened when the driver said, "It's perfect, Pappy. What did she run?"

"A hair over 191," the crew chief answered.

"That means I can do 192 tomorrow. That should win the pole."

"*Will* win the pole," Pappy corrected.

"Let's not count our chickens," David said, smiling at the man's exuberance.

Beth took a stenographer's pad from her purse and made a note. "Oh, we're just chatting right now," David said. "This isn't for print. The track could be real hot tomorrow and I might not run as fast as I did today. A lot of things can happen."

Beth shrugged and marked through her notation. She was covering an arcane sport. She had a lot to learn, and she wanted to share what she learned with her readers. Everyone knew how it was to hit a baseball or shoot a basketball, but how was it to drive a race car? She asked David, explaining that she'd like to make notes and use the information in a feature story someday. She told him she drove a red Miata, and that it was about as far removed from a Winston Cup stock car as an automobile could be.

"There are two main elements to racing," he said. "Speed and competition. Speed is exhilarating. If you've ever kicked your little red Miata up to a hundred miles an hour on the interstate you know that. And I'll bet you have. I'll bet you've seen the speedometer needle on a hundred—probably just for a moment—and had that feeling of breaking the bounds of normalcy. Right?"

"One time," Beth answered, smiling. "And it was just for a moment, because I was afraid I'd see a blinking blue light in my rearview mirror. It was on I-65 between Montgomery and Birmingham. I felt deliciously evil. It was, as you say, as if I'd slipped the bounds of routine existence."

"Okay, imagine there's no danger of a blinking blue light, and you can drive a hundred miles an hour for as long as you want to."

"Great," she answered.

"Now imagine you've pushed the hundred miles an hour to one-ninety-one. Remember how it was to go a hundred in your Miata and imagine seeing the speedometer needle—just for a moment—resting on one-ninety-one."

"I wouldn't like that," Beth said.

"Then we're beginning to separate the race drivers from the civilians. Plenty of folks would get a thrill out of a hundred; practically everyone would be terrified on one-ninety-one. As Neil Bonnett once said,

'When I was a pipe fitter there were a lot of people wanting my job, but not many want the job of driving my car at Talladega.' But I thrive on driving a race car that fast, and not just for a moment but for three hours. I love it."

David smiled. He knew that 191 miles an hour had registered with Beth not just as a statistic on a qualifying sheet but as a terrifying reality.

"Okay, let's go back to one hundred miles an hour, and you're having fun," he said, "but let's imagine forty-two other Miatas on the track, and you're all dueling for position. You have to stick your car into a hole between two others, and there's only a couple of feet to spare."

"Count me out," Beth said.

"That's called competition," David said, "and it's the other main element in my racing addiction—and make no mistake, it is an addiction. I'm in competition with other drivers and with the track itself, just as a golfer is in competition with other golfers and the course itself—though the penalty for a mistake usually is considerably more severe in racing. I delight in passing a faster car in the corner because I set up the pass perfectly. I delight in running optimum lap after optimum lap at crazy old Darlington, even in practice.

"Cale Yarborough said driving a race car is like dancing with a chain saw. I'm gratified by the knowledge that I'm one of a small number of humans who can drive a race car fast and competitively—who can dance with a chain saw.

"In fact, I once watched a fellow juggling three chain saws on TV. I think I know the satisfaction he felt. He did what others not only couldn't do, they wouldn't dare attempt it."

Beth made up her mind to drive her Miata a hundred miles an hour again—but only for a moment, and only if no other cars were in sight.

"Chili time, hon," David said, motioning for her to follow him. Pappy swung open the back door of the tractor-trailer, disappeared inside, and returned with a sack of groceries under each arm, which he handed to David. Then he went back for more.

The crew chief set up a gas burner in the garage, spread the contents of the sacks on the workbench, and began mixing them in a big steel pot. "You've never eaten chili until you've eaten Pappy's," David said, draping his arm around Beth's shoulder.

"Oh, I'm full," she said. "I had lunch with Mr. Lanston."

David withdrew his arm and without a word headed for the race car hauler to change clothes.

Chapter 3

When he returned, wearing his street clothes, David ignored her. He pretended to concentrate on Pappy Draper's blending of the ingredients into chili. When she attempted conversation he answered in clipped sentences. Finally, embarrassed, Beth said, "I've got to scrape up some kind of feature this afternoon. See you folks."

"Okay," David said, his eyes riveted on the blue flame of the burner.

She had walked perhaps ten feet when she heard Pappy say, "I'd better get some water," and he fell into step behind her.

"Don't mind David," he whispered. "It's just that he and Lanston strike sparks."

"Well, he needn't take it out on me," Beth said. "I'd never even heard of Herman Lanston before today—and my first impression is that his manners are better than David Marlow's."

"I'll tell David you just met Lanston," Pappy said.

"I don't have to explain anything to David Marlow about Herman Lanston," she sniffed—but secretly she was pleased that Pappy would mention it to David.

The crew chief stopped by a spigot. "See you at qualifying tomorrow," he said. "And don't be too hard on David."

"Bye, Pappy."

Beth busied herself with admiring the racing machines, touching the so-called stock cars that were polished until they were as slick as mercury to give them every possible edge over the wall of air they must displace. She hoped by looking and listening that an idea for a feature would pop into her mind.

"Miss Barrett," a voice said, and she turned to see Vern Parchman. He was smiling, forcing himself to be cordial. "I have a scoop for you."

Scoop. It was a word the public, not reporters, used. And Beth knew intuitively that Herman Lanston had reprimanded his driver for his earlier curt manner and sent him to her wearing this phony smile. The two thoughts made Beth want to grin, but she bit the inside of her lower lip. Besides, who was she to look a gift scoop in the mouth on her first day at the track. "Fine," she said.

"Follow me," Parchman said, and he was off in a lope, Beth on his heels.

Uh oh, she thought when she realized he was headed for Lanston's motor home. "Mr. Parchman, can we . . ." But already he was opening the door. Beth looked into the big rear view mirror on the side of the motor home and saw David watching her from beside his car.

"It's quiet in here," Parchman said, motioning for her to sit. "What would you like? There's a refrigerator full of anything you want to drink."

"Yes, I know," she said. "Nothing, please."

Parchman opened a soft drink and sprawled on the bench opposite her. "Here's your scoop: I'm retiring after this season. I'm predicting here and now that I'll win my third straight Winston Cup championship. And after I do, I'll hang up my helmet for good."

That was a scoop, all right, the kind a driver or car owner would reserve for a reporter to whom he owed a big favor. The announcement that Vern Parchman was driving his last season would without question be the lead story in the sports section of *The Birmingham News* tomorrow. She knew Vern Parchman had no regard for a female sports writer, so he had to be acting on Herman Lanston's orders. Did Lanston feel badly about denying her the interview with himself? Did he simply wish to see a young woman make an impressive splash into a new beat? Whatever the reason, Beth pictured the slack jaws of the chauvinists back at the paper when they saw her report, and the prospect pleased her.

Beth pitched into the interview, and Parchman gave her lively quotes, framing his words for the most dramatic effect. "I'll even predict that I'll win the pole position in qualifying tomorrow," he said. "Why stop there? I'll win the race Sunday."

They completed the interview and Parchman excused himself to practice. Beth poured herself a glass of lemonade, but she was so eager to begin writing the story that she forgot to drink it.

BETH WAS DREAMING of race cars on an assembly line in a mysterious plant, a mannequin resembling David Marlow being installed behind the steering wheel of every other one, the others receiving Vern Parchman mannequins, when the telephone rang.

"Yep?" she said sleepily, glancing around the motel room, at first forgetting where she was.

"I just read your story," Blake Watkins said. "Hell of a piece. Only thing, what're you going to do for encores the next forty years?"

The story. Yes. *Please get off the phone, Blake, so I can buy a paper and see the story.*

"Thanks," she said. "I just got lucky."

"I'm a genius," Watkins said. "I put a woman on the racing beat, she goes to Talladega and sleeps with the champion the first day, and he gives her an exclusive."

"That's not funny, Blake," Beth said, yawning.

"Seriously, congratulations. I'm glad you're a member of my staff, Beth."

"So am I. You're nice to call."

She hung up, hit the floor, found a quarter and a dime in her purse, slipped on a robe, and went outside barefoot. She spotted a *Birmingham News* rack, inserted thirty-five cents, and turned to the sports pages before she returned to her room. The headline stretched all the way across the top of the lead page: *Champion driver Parchman calling it a career after this season.* Boxed into the story was the message A *NEWS* EXCLUSIVE.

She glanced at the first column, at the words she never tired of reading: By Beth Barrett, *News* staff writer. And today her byline was atop the biggest story of her career.

An old woman glanced disapprovingly at the barefoot, disheveled thing with the Dutch boy haircut. "Good morning!" Beth shot at her.

She returned to her room and read the story, savoring each word. *Thank you, Herman Lanston, for this one.* But her thoughts were interrupted by a photo under the story. It showed David climbing from the window of his car after his practice run. She wanted to share her good fortune with David. The old days suddenly passed on the screen of her mind, David winning on a dirt track, then pressing her to him, as if by doing so he could more intimately share with her his joy of victory, his satisfaction in knowing he had taken one more step toward his goal.

The track would open at 9 A.M. and she wanted to be there when it did, to explain to David the importance such a story could have in her career. Her watch said 7:20. Darn, that was a long time to wait.

She showered, ate breakfast, read the paper. Finally, out of patience, she drove the few miles to the speedway and parked outside the gate. Twenty minutes later hers was the first car admitted.

The garage was eerily quiet. Where there had been the cacophony of motors being revved the day before, the only sounds were those of mechanics saying their good mornings as they reported for work.

A half-hour later David and his team hadn't arrived. Well, she supposed, when you were already dialed in, there was no point in showing up while the dew was still on the grass.

Finally she saw David's car roll through the gate. David and a man on the passenger side were chatting, and David didn't see her. She touched the sports page that she had rolled up and jammed into the hip pocket of her jeans in case he hadn't seen it.

David parked and got out, and she smiled and waved to him. Then her smile disappeared when his companion slammed the other door.

It was Charlie Murphy.

He wore a green satin, lettered shirt and a matching cap. He smirked when he saw Beth, but he walked toward her.

"Charlie," she said.

"Miss Barrett."

She read the words on his shirt: *Penderton Tools Racing Team.* He obviously delighted in her puzzled look.

"You and Watkins couldn't run me out of racing," he said. "A fellow doesn't cover the sport for more than a quarter of a century and not make contacts. Alex Penderton owed me; now I'm the flack for his Winston Cup team."

"The flack?"

"Media relations man. Anything I can do to serve the press? But, judging from your story this morning, you seem to be serving yourself pretty well."

She felt guilt at having taken Murphy's job, though she knew she wasn't responsible. "You quit the paper, Charlie, after all those years?"

"You're brokenhearted, aren't you?" he said facetiously.

She had tried to be friends with him for four years and it hadn't worked. Why bother now? "Frankly, it doesn't matter one way or the other to me," Beth said.

She stepped by him and approached David. "Morning, Dirt Dauber," she said brightly.

"Hello, Beth." His voice was without inflection.

"What do you think of Parchman's decision to quit after this season?" she asked, fishing for a compliment on her story.

"No comment."

"I wasn't asking as a reporter, David. I was just saying good morning. Pardon me if I'm still happy because I got an exclusive."

"I suppose Lanston can give a story to whomever he chooses," David said dryly. "If it helps you along, congratulations."

"What in the world is wrong with you?"

David removed his helmet from its bag and brushed imaginary dust from it. "Look, Beth, this speedway is my office today, and I've got to go to work. I should think you would consider it your office, too. Let's be professional about it."

She was mortified. "You got it, Mr. Marlow," she said, turning on her heel and disappearing behind a truck.

She stopped, out of sight of anyone, and fought back a tear. So David had changed. She *was* merely someone he had known in the past. Now he was a star, with all the egotistical, specious ramifications of the word. She would have bet that fame and money wouldn't have done this to the guy who used to laugh at his own mud-caked face in the rearview mirror.

What did she care? David had been the companion of a college freshman, a girl to whom a lost lipstick was a crisis. Now the girl was a woman, a reporter with the biggest newspaper in Alabama. Times change. People change. Forget him and go to work.

But even as she tried to don this emotional armor she realized the truth. The disruption caused her to admit it to herself for the first time, as in the face of an approaching tornado a dullard in a classroom might admit to herself for the first time that she really did cherish her schoolhouse. The truth was that she had loved David, only David, and that she had never stopped. Overwhelmed by the inexorable circumstances of his pursuit of ambition and her pursuit of education, she had succeeded in submerging that love, but it hadn't ended. She had watched him leave for Virginia and had told herself that it was merely a case of one of many boyfriends she would have in her life going his own way, that was all. But no man in the seven years since then had interested her; she usually preferred to stay in her apartment and read rather than to date, and when she did date, the man was chosen carefully so that a romantic entanglement would be unthinkable.

Now she was hurting, the admission to herself of her love for David rubbing salt in the wound caused by the daggers of his words. She had to get hold of herself—and she would, by plunging into her work.

"Excuse me, are you Arnie Shale?" she asked a young man who was passing by.

"Right," he said cheerily.

"I'm Beth Barrett of *The Birmingham News*. I notice you're leading the Rookie of the Year standings. Could we chat for a few minutes?"

"Sure," he said, brushing a boyish swatch of brown hair from his forehead. "My tow car's over there in the shade. The air conditioner died three summers ago, but it'll be better than standing here in the sun."

He opened the passenger-side door of the old car and Beth sat on threadbare upholstery. Tools were sprawled in disarray across the back seat. She glanced at the odometer: 96,788.

"Coming up on two hundred thousand, huh?" she said confidentially.

"How do you know it isn't one hundred thousand?" Arnie Shale whispered, as if it were a secret.

"I had a . . . friend who had a car somewhat like this," she said. "It succumbed just before two hundred thousand."

"Oh, Lordy," the boy said, gasping, holding his heart. "Don't tell me that. When this thing's gone I'll have to buy a plow line and throw it over my shoulder and pull my trailer and racer by foot."

Beth liked him. He momentarily got her mind off David. "First, how old are you, Arnie?" she asked, pencil poised over a stenographer's pad.

"I'm nineteen."

"And what is somebody so young doing on the Winston Cup circuit?"

"Trying to make a name for myself while my whiskers are still downy," he said. "This is all I ever wanted to do."

"Obviously, you aren't driving for one of the big-buck teams, but how does a nineteen-year-old get a Winston Cup car at all?"

"That's my racer over there in the end space," he said. "Does it look unusual?"

Beth squinted and saw a white Ford with small black marks on it. "What are those?" she asked.

"They're signatures. I'm from Springville, Alabama, and my car is the *St. Clair County Special*. I knew I couldn't find a big sponsor, so I sold the idea of everybody in the county chipping in a little something to pay the bills, and signing their names or the names of their businesses on the car. That way an ordinary fellow becomes a car owner, and he's got a stake in the race."

The names of service stations, junkyards, garages, restaurants, banks, sporting goods stores, florists, video stores, and individuals were signed wherever they would fit. "What's this?" Beth asked, pointing to the name *Hand Me Downs*.

"It's a children's clothing store in the village of Argo," Arnie said, "The lady's a racing fan, and she gave me a couple of hundred bucks and said if I ever got married and had young'uns she'd keep clothes on their backs. It'll be a long time before that happens, though, because I'm married to racing."

The race car itself looked as sleek as any of the others, Beth remarked.

"I bought one of David Marlow's old cars, and me and my cousin Paul do the mechanical work. We stay in cheap motels or"—she saw the embarrassment in his reddening cheeks—"in our old tent. The folks in the campgrounds at the different speedways like having a driver among them. We eat a lot of hot dogs, but sometimes the fans will share whatever they're barbecuing. We can always find a few guys in every town who've done some short-tracking, and they'll handle pit stops for us for nothing, just to say they did it."

In his eyes Beth saw the same determination she had once seen in David's. She found herself patting him on the hand. "Despite all these difficulties, you're leading in Rookie of the Year standings," she said. "That's amazing."

"I drive over my head a lot," Arnie said. "That's the only way you'll ever make it in Winston Cup—do something to get noticed. I don't mean win a race; I couldn't win one of those things with my equipment. I mean stay in the same lap with the leaders for half the race, outrun a car that everybody knows is better than yours, stick the nose of your racer in a tight spot to win one more position, something like that.

"Look, there are guys out here who make a good living and never in their careers win a race. Some of them are content to do that. An independent like me—that's what they call a fellow without a big sponsor—has to be careful not to get himself typecast with that group. So in every race I try to show whoever might be watching that, hey, maybe Arnie Shale hasn't got a prayer of winning, but it makes a difference to him whether he finishes twenty-fourth or twenty-fifth, the same difference it makes to a star like David Marlow whether he finishes first or finishes second. Maybe I have to be one of the worst right now, but at least I can be the best of the worst."

She could have closed her eyes and been hearing the David Marlow whose face was caked with mud, Beth thought. "I hope you get what you want, Arnie," she said softly.

"When I get rich I'll buy you a new pencil," she said, pointing at the stub that moved across the page of her steno pad and laughing, obviously a bit embarrassed by the speech he had just given.

Beth interviewed Arnie Shale for nearly an hour. She learned he'd plowed for neighbors to make enough money to buy a six-cylinder amateur car for the dirt tracks before he even had a driver's license. He raced it three seasons and now he was in Winston Cup. The leap was the equivalent of that from a high school team to the National Football League. She sensed a recklessness about his ambition. At least David had driven in the middle divisions of Sportsman and Grand National, climbing a ladder to Winston Cup.

She was thumbing through her notes, wondering if there were any more questions, when the boy startled her with, "Would you go to the party with me tonight? There's a party for the drivers at an antebellum mansion near here."

She wished the words were coming from David's lips. "I'm sorry, I can't," she said.

He nodded. "Well, I've got to go practice. I can only afford the tires for about three laps of dialing in, so I'll be back in a jiffy if you think of anything else."

"Thanks, Arnie. I believe I have it all."

Beth strolled through the garage, avoiding glancing toward David's space. She introduced herself to some mechanics, and one flattered her with, "Oh, yeah, you're the gir . . . woman who had the story on Parchman quitting in today's paper. Interesting."

She felt a hand on her shoulder. "It *was* interesting," a voice said. "Good piece of reporting."

Beth turned and smiled back at the dancing eyes of Herman Lanston "It's hard to drop a fly ball that falls right into your glove," she said. "Thanks. I appreciate it."

"There's a price tag," Lanston said, winking.

"There usually is."

"The payment is an easy one. Would you accompany me to a party tonight? It's held at a nearby mansion, and it's always quite pleasant, a trip back in time to the old South."

Not as easy as you believe, Beth thought, aching at the notion of going to a party with anyone but David, especially one that David probably would attend. And she had just turned down Arnie Shale's invitation. It would be embarrassing to see Arnie there.

But Lanston had given her an important story, and she supposed she did owe him this. And he was a man of style, far from boring.

"Okay," she said.

Chapter 4

*T*he afternoon produced clouds that cooled the asphalt of Talladega Superspeedway and brought grins to the faces of Pappy Draper and the other crew chiefs. "Qualifying speeds will be up," Draper told Beth. "Everybody in the world hopes for a nice sunny day except racers, and we want clouds. Makes us sound like creatures out of Transylvania, doesn't it?"

Draper had walked halfway across the garage area to speak to her. Obviously, it bothered him that David had been so curt. He liked Beth, but he worshipped David, and the kindly man was disturbed by the position in which he found himself.

"Who'll be your chief competition in qualifying?" Beth asked.

"Vern Parchman. He's always everybody's chief competition in anything. Lanston shovels the money into their operation, and Vern is a good driver. They're tough."

Arnie Shale's car was the first onto the track. Each driver would be permitted two laps, the faster lap to count as his qualifying speed. The speeds would determine the starting order for the five-hundred-miler.

Shale's best lap was 186.011 miles per hour. "That will get him in the field," Draper said, "but he'll be way back."

A dozen others qualified before David Marlow's white Ford pulled onto the track to the applause of the crowd in the double-decked grandstand.

"I hope he wins the pole," Beth told Draper.

The car disappeared behind infield buildings, its speed increasing, and when David took the green flag for his first lap of qualifying, Beth squeezed her fists until they turned white. How could anyone have the courage to drive one of those things?

Yells and whistles mixed with the roar of the engine when the public address announcer called David's speed at the completion of the first lap: 192.124. The second lap speed was almost identical: 192.121.

"See you later, Beth!" Draper said, laughing and sprinting toward the entrance in the pit wall where David would momentarily make his appearance.

His car turned into the garage area, engine shut off, coasting to a stop. Beth lagged behind, letting a corps of reporters form a semicircle outside the driver's window, from which David would exit.

TV cameras rolled and microphones were shoved under his nose as both feet hit the asphalt.

"It was a good run," David said without being asked. "It was better than anything we'd done in practice, but I knew we had something in reserve."

"How's the car handling?" someone asked.

"It's excellent. Pappy Draper and the boys have everything in perfect order. We tested here last week and that helped."

David wouldn't look her way. She decided she would force him.

"Will that speed be enough to win the pole?" she asked.

"I believe Vern Parchman is the only one who might beat it," David said dryly. "But I'm sure you know that."

Why would I know it? Beth thought, but this was no time for an argument.

The questions continued for several minutes, then David excused himself.

"The next qualifier is Vern Parchman," the public address announcer said, and Beth saw Herman Lanston's blue Chevrolet roll onto the track.

And Herman Lanston stationed himself at her side.

"Mr. Marlow is going to be in for a rude awakening," he said.

"What?"

"He has been considerably faster than us in practice, but Vern has just been toying with him."

Lanston's charm always evaporated when David was the subject. Clearly, a deep dislike separated the two men.

Parchman completed his first lap; the fans in the grandstand and the racing teams in the garage were silent as they waited for the public address announcer's pronouncement. Finally, he said 190.577 miles an hour. Beth glanced at the speed she had written for David in her notebook: 192.124. She forced herself to remain poker-faced in Lanston's presence.

Lanston pointed to Pappy Draper, who was patting another mechanic on the back. "Watch that grin melt after this lap," he said.

Parchman's car raced out of the fourth turn, by the garage, and over the finish line, as steady as if it were on a rail. "Listen to this one, race fans!" the announcer blurted. "Vern Parchman just ran 194.223 miles an hour!"

Indeed, Draper's grin did melt.

"How could he be that much faster on the second lap?" Beth asked Lanston.

"He let up on the first lap, just to make them think they probably had the pole," Lanston yelled over the cheers of his mechanics.

For the first time, she realized Lanston didn't merely dislike David; he hated him. And he wanted her readers to know he'd pull such a trick, too.

"Why do you have it in for David Marlow?" Beth asked.

"He walked out on me in the middle of a season," Lanston said. "But that's a long story. Why don't you go interview the pole winner?"

Parchman climbed from his car and was surrounded by reporters. He laughed heartily at something one of them said. Beth joined them, and as she did she glanced at David's garage stall. His hand was on Pappy

Draper's shoulder and he obviously was consoling the older man, whose head was down.

"Did I ever doubt I'd win the pole?" Parchman repeated a reporter's question. "If you had read Miss Barrett's story in *The Birmingham News* this morning you'd have known I predicted I'd win it. Right, Miss Barrett?"

The other writers and broadcasters turned to the only woman in their midst. "Right," she said, with a sigh.

BETH FILED HER story, interviewed a driver for an off-beat feature, took a swim in the motel pool, treated herself to a leisurely hot bath, put on a bright yellow dress, and waited for Herman Lanston.

She thought about what Lanston had told her, that David walked out in the middle of the season. That could be disastrous for a racing team. Money is invested, cars are built, there are salaries to be paid—and, suddenly, no driver.

But in her mind's eye she couldn't see David doing such a thing without a reason. Of course, she told herself, she couldn't picture David treating her as he was, either.

There was a knock at her door, and she opened it to Herman Lanston. He wore an expensive white linen suit, a lime shirt, and a white silk tie. "Hello, my dear," he said.

The malevolent look she had seen in his eyes at the speedway had been replaced by the kind, concerned gaze that had impressed her when she met him. "Mr. Lanston, you look as cool as an ice cream cone," she said."And you look as radiant as a yellow tulip, which I might add is an appropriate description of a beauty who wears her hair in a Dutch boy cut."

He led her to his car, a low-slung yellow convertible. "What kind of car is it?" Beth asked.

"A Ferrari," Lanston said, opening the door for her. "It will run one hundred and fifty miles an hour—and then some."

"Not with me in it," Beth said.

They drove over the undulating Alabama countryside, Lanston expertly controlling the superb car at a speed too fast for comfort. But that was all right; Beth enjoyed the ride, enjoyed the responses of a great automobile on the curvy road.

They topped a hill and Lanston downshifted and braked. "There it is," he said.

Beth saw a handsome white antebellum home, its columns alabaster sentinels guarding a graceful way of life that had almost vanished. Cars were parked on the lawn alongside the house, and the mansion was reflected in their finishes, ghostly in the soft moonlight.

"There must be a message in this somewhere," Lanston said, tucking the Ferrari behind a BMW. "One of the world's fastest cars parked beside a house that was built before automobiles were invented."

The host, a racing fan who owned and farmed more than two thousand acres of land, waved from the porch. "Herman, welcome! Get in here before these drivers drink up all the bourbon and branch."

Beth met the old man, who pronounced her the prettiest sports writer in the world. He then led them into the huge living room, where her eyes met Arnie Shale's. "Excuse me, gentlemen," she said, and she crossed the room to where he stood.

"How are you, Arnie?" she asked.

He didn't smile. "Okay."

"Arnie, I really didn't intend to come to the party," she whispered, "but I owe Mr. Lanston a favor for the Parchman story, and this repays it. I hope you understand."

His eyes brightened. "I do. Can I get you a drink?"

Beth sipped white wine and glanced around the room. The original wide, polished planks of the floor were uncarpeted, proud reminders that feet wearing the slippers of a more slowly paced time had once trod them. The crystal prisms of a chandelier that had been converted to electricity transformed the light into the colors of the spectrum. The room was furnished with antiques, and velvet reached from the top of high windows.

Her thoughts drifted to a similar house in Tuscaloosa. When she was a student at the University of Alabama, her sorority held a party there. She invited David, and she remembered tears welling in her eyes because he had to buy a suit on credit since he didn't own one. The night had been much as this one, moonlit, cool but not unpleasant. The fragrance of magnolias had ridden on the breeze as David had taken her hand and led her into the shadows on the lawn, where he kissed her with uncommon tenderness.

But that was the David of the past. The David of today was a star.

Beth saw a matron punch her husband's shoulder and point toward the door, and Beth turned to see the David of today arriving.

He wore a light blue jacket, white shirt, and white tie. His black hair had recovered from the mussing his helmet had given it at the track. Beth saw his dark eyes gazing kindly on those of an excited middle-aged woman who was being introduced to him.

"I see the number two qualifier has arrived." Herman Lanston had rejoined her.

"Mr. Lanston, this is Arnie Shale," Beth said, glad for an opportunity to change the subject. "Herman Lanston."

Arnie gulped. "My pleasure, sir," he said. "I've admired your race cars since I was a kid."

"Which seems like only yesterday," Lanston said, embarrassing the youngster.

"I guess so," Arnie muttered.

"Well, who knows? Maybe you'll have a chance to drive for me some day. Parchman and the rest of the stars weren't always stars."

"That would be great, Mr. Lanston. I believe I could really give Miss Barrett something to write about if I was in your car."

Beth smiled at the boy. "I believe you would, Arnie," she said.

"I hope it happens."

"Parchman's quitting after this year," Lanston said. "Show me something in the race Sunday."

"I'll do it or break my neck trying," Arnie pledged.

When the rookie had left them, Beth said, "He's so deserving. I'm glad you'd consider him to drive for you."

"But of course I wouldn't," Lanston said, laughing. "He's years and years away from driving for me—probably a lifetime away."

"He believed you," Beth said. "So did I."

"It was merely conversation," Lanston said, impatience in his voice. "Let's not talk racing. I want to hear about you."

Beth felt put off by the little charade, but she related a synopsis of her life story, Lanston attentively taking in every word, his unwavering gaze slightly unnerving her. She was glad when the host summoned Lanston to a corner to answer a farm-related question.

"Nice place," she heard Pappy Draper's raspy voice say. She turned to see him at her side. David was with him, obviously towed into her company against his will.

"Hello, Beth," he said.

"David."

"Excuse me a minute, folks," Pappy said, pretending it was urgent he speak to a driver across the room.

"You'll have a front-row starting position Sunday," Beth said to David.

"Not the one I wanted, though. Your man Parchman saw to that."

"My man Parchman?"

"We're all adults here," David said. "What you do is your business, Beth. In fact, congratulations."

Sudden anger seethed inside her. "David, you and I once were . . . well, something more than friends. I came to the race track looking forward to seeing you again. And I thought you were pleased to see me. Now it's as if you never even knew me. What's the problem?"

"There's no problem, Beth," he answered. "As I said, we're all adults. What you do, the people you associate with, are your business."

"Are you talking about Herman Lanston? Just because there's a bone of contention between you and Herman Lanston, I'm not supposed to speak to him? Is that it? Well, if it is, you're absolutely right: the people I associate with *are* my business."

"Then I'd say we're in total agreement," David replied icily.

"What happened to the sensitive, wonderful guy who used to drive the dirt tracks?" Beth said, almost in a whisper. "Boy, your determination to get to the top has gotten out of hand. Do you know what I think, David? I think that Parchman is the champion, and it's eating you alive that you aren't. You hate Parchman and Lanston because they're where you want to be. There's a simple name for it. It's called jealousy."

"Is the lecture over?" David asked.

"It wasn't intended to be a lecture. It's just that something that was precious to me has gone awry. I'm dumbfounded that Parchman and Lanston are under your skin to the extent that you'd turn a cold shoulder to me because I'm friendly with them."

"Excuse me," David said, and he walked away.

Lanston rejoined her. "That was getting heated," he said. "Mr. Marlow apparently roused your ire."

"Can we leave, Herman?" Beth said. She couldn't stand to remain there in that house, under the same roof with David, love for him and distaste for his behavior vying with each other in her overwhelmed mind.

"Did he insult you? I'll . . ."

"No, he didn't insult me. Please, let's go."

Lanston apologized to the host, saying Beth had a headache, and soon they were riding over the country roads, moonlight peeping through the heavy limbs of the longleaf pines. She had asked him to put the top down, but no winds raked through the convertible. A sheet of tissue in her lap didn't move. She could see the stars, but she was secluded from the elements. Beth felt better, as if she were secure in a cocoon, the trouble with David part of an outside world that didn't have to be faced until a distant point in time. She closed her eyes and reclined her head on the Ferrari's headrest.

"I'm glad you're on the racing beat," Lanston said, breaking the silence of several minutes.

"So am I," Beth answered, but she wondered if she really was glad. Before Blake Watkins called her into his office to announce the promotion, her life had been pleasantly even, her work gratifying, her love for David on the back burner. Now she ached because of what she had seen David become, a man who allowed their relationship to become warped by petty jealousy more likely to be found in a school boy.

Or was it that simple? That answer was too pat, Beth thought as the Ferrari facilely negotiated a sharp turn. She believed she knew David better than that. Yet, in the absence of any other answer, what was she supposed to think?

"You're quieter than the night," Lanston said.

"I'm sorry," Beth replied. She knew she wasn't being fair to the man. She had taken him from the party and now she was boring him. "Tell me all about yourself," she said. "I may pry that story from you yet."

"No newspaper story," Lanston said, "but I will put you to sleep with the epic of my life. I was born and raised in an average middle class family in California. I attempted to race on the short tracks and found I was totally unsuited for it. So I . . ."

"You don't handle this car as if you were unsuited for it," Beth said. "We just took that turn at seventy-eight miles an hour without a bobble."

Lanston chuckled. "This is a Ferrari 360 Spider F1. It costs more than $200,000. For that kind of money one expects a machine that will help keep him out of the ditches. Give the credit to the car, not to me."

"I still think it requires skill, but go on," Beth said.

"An uncle had a cannery that was on shaky ground because of

mismanagement. It was headed for a bankruptcy, and I offered to save it in exchange for controlling interest."

"Save it? How?"

"By instituting some sound business practices. I thought I could make it a financial success through common sense and ingenuity. I was right, and now many, many housewives each day open a can of vegetables with the Lanston Farms label.

"When the company began making money I started sponsoring a short-track racing team. If I couldn't drive one of the darn things to Victory Lane, at least I could help someone else do it and have the satisfaction of seeing my name on the car.

"After Lanston Farms really began prospering, I bought a Winston Cup team. There's an old rhyme that says the only difference in men and boys is the price of their toys. I suppose that's true, but racing goes beyond that with me. It's my passion. I don't let anything stand in the way of my car winning races and my driver being the seasonal champion. If my crew chief tells me a hundred thousand dollars will enable him to find a tenth of a mile an hour more, he gets the hundred thousand dollars.

"But it's my money, and I insist on waving the baton. If I tell Vern Parchman to climb the flagpole during the singing of the National Anthem before a race, then I expect him to start shinnying.

"David Marlow and I could have set records over the years that would never have been approached by any other team, but he committed the unpardonable sin of forgetting who was boss. He insulted me by walking out in midseason.

"David is the greatest talent in the game, but it is a team sport, just as surely as football is a team sport. He can't do it alone. I hire the best crew chief, the best engine builders, the best chassis men, the best janitor, the best everything.

"I do owe David my gratitude, though. When he quit my team he added a dimension to the pleasure I receive from racing. Now I not only am gratified by winning, I am gratified by beating David Marlow."

That was a revealing speech, Beth thought. There was a hard, perhaps cruel, side to this man who could be so charming. Despite her anger and dismay at David's treatment of her, she felt uneasy knowing he was Herman Lanston's enemy.

She sensed an opportunity to learn the details of their split—but she was disappointed. "It's a long story, one better left untold on a fine October night," Lanston answered her query.

"You didn't mention your wife," Beth said. "How long have you been a widower?"

"Oh, three years, I guess."

Beth waited. Lanston was silent.

"What was her name? Did she like racing?"

"Louise. It's still painful for me to speak of her. See the moonlight on the lake? It looks like white silk."

Beth had run up two conversational blind alleys. She chose a lighter subject. "I wonder how it would feel to travel a hundred and ninety-four miles an hour in a car," she said.

"I don't know," Lanston said, "but I can show you how it feels to go one-fifty."

"What do you mean?"

"I told you this car would do one-fifty. Are you interested in finding out?"

"And I told you I wouldn't be in it," she said. But suddenly, inexplicably, the idea appealed to her. Had some of the lure of danger in the sport she was covering rubbed off on her? She was surprised to hear herself say, "Let's do go one-fifty."

Lanston laughed and turned the car sharply. "We'll drive over to Speedway Boulevard. It's the straight road that runs in front of the track. It's perfect."

Excitement replaced the melancholy that David's snub had caused. It was a stupid thing to do, riding on a public road at such a speed, but she'd just call it backgrounding for her new beat.

They turned onto Speedway Boulevard, and Lanston drove by the dark hulk of the track at a normal speed. "I want to check out the road and be sure it's clear," he said.

He made a U-turn in front of a little church, slammed the lever into first gear, and stomped the accelerator pedal. Beth's head popped back and they were on their way. "I love it so much that I had this car flown in by cargo plane from my home in California just so I could drive it this week," he said.

The speedometer needle moved rapidly, past a hundred, past one-ten, past one-twenty-five. The trees beside the road were a blur. Beth wanted to close her eyes but she forced herself to gape all about her, to record in her mind every sensation.

Finally, after less than two miles, the needle touched one-fifty. "There it is," Lanston said, teasing her by removing both hands from the wheel. "Fun?"

"It's great," Beth shouted above the whine of the engine. "Dumb, but great."

Lanston lifted his foot and the car began to slow. They were coasting at ninety miles an hour when Beth saw the blue light in the rearview mirror. "Uh oh," Lanston said.

He stopped the Ferrari in the gravel alongside the road and the state trooper's car parked behind it. Lanston rolled down the window and impatiently tapped his fingertips on the sill.

"Driver's license," the trooper growled.

He read the inscription on the license in the beam of his flashlight. "Mr. Lanston, another trooper car was parked back up the road, and he clocked you on radar at more than a hundred and forty miles an hour. Maybe you pull stunts like that back in California, but you don't do it in Alabama. You're going to jail."

Ouch, Beth thought. *Wait until Blake Watkins hears about this.*

Unruffled, Lanston opened his wallet. "Shine that light here," he told the trooper, who looked at him quizzically but obeyed.

Lanston withdrew two five-hundred-dollar bills from a compartment in the wallet. The trooper's eyes bugged.

"One for you, one for your buddy back up the road," Lanston said.

"Uh . . . uh . . . gosh," the trooper stammered. "Well, you folks have a nice evening. Try to slow it down a little." He tucked the money into his shirt pocket, shuffled back to his car, and drove away.

Suddenly Beth felt very uneasy in the presence of Herman Lanston. She felt ashamed of whatever she may have contributed to the scenario that had just passed. "I've got a long day tomorrow," she said. "I think I'd better go back to the motel and read myself to sleep."

Lanston drove at the speed limit of sixty-five and turned into the parking lot of her motel. He opened the car door for her and started walking with her to her room. "There's no point in you climbing those steps," Beth said. "I enjoyed this evening. Good night."

But Lanston never hesitated. "I'd like to come in for a nightcap," he said.

"I don't have anything to drink."

"That doesn't matter. I'd like to come in."

They stood at her door. "I'll see you at the speedway tomorrow," Beth said.

Lanston looked into her eyes as if trying to decide whether to pursue the matter. Finally he said, "Okay. I'll visit another night."

Beth unlocked the door and with relief closed and locked it. She heard Herman Lanston's footsteps grow fainter, and then she heard the Ferrari's engine come to life.

She closed her eyes and leaned her forehead on the door. Why couldn't it have been David who wanted to come into her room?

Chapter 5

*B*eth's motel nestled beside Lake Logan Martin, which provided thousands of acres to boaters and fishermen, and she walked barefoot through the dewy grass to the edge of the water. Waves slapped against the red clay of the bank, dispatched there by the departing boat of a couple of early rising anglers. The growl of its outboard motor lessened as it skimmed across the surface, and finally it was but a dot on the horizon.

Daylight had just broken but Beth couldn't sleep, so she had slipped into her jeans and shirt, poured black coffee from the little coffee maker in her room, and now she watched the blue mist rise off the lake. Lithe waterbirds skipped off the surface like black arrows, having their morning feed. A family of brown ducks passed in formation at her feet, tame, hoping she would be one of those motel guests who tossed them food.

Saturday was devoted to a minor-league race for Automobile Racing Club of America drivers. Blake Watkins wanted a concise twelve-inch story on the event, for it was football day in Alabama and the games would dominate newspaper space. She'd cover the ARCA race, write an advance on Sunday's five-hundred-miler, and she'd be finished. She decided to relax at lakeside and then read in her room. She wanted to avoid even seeing David, and the less time she spent at the speedway, the easier that would be.

A bass broke the surface of the lake—now becoming golden with the rising of the morning sun—and then vanished. Almost as suddenly had David's attention to her disappeared. He had been excited to see her, she knew that, but he had turned cold the same day. The obvious explanation was that a celebrity's fragile ego was wounded by her friendliness with Herman Lanston, a man he hated, and that he was reacting by pouting like a child.

But one learned in the newspaper business that obvious explanations often were incorrect ones. She believed pieces were missing from this puzzle, but she didn't know where to look for them. Her brain was swirling with the confusion concerning David and from the pressure of her new beat. Her coverage of the qualifying had been disappointing because she had allowed herself to become emotionally involved in Parchman's taking the pole from David. Her story had been wooden, tentative. She had not followed the exclusive story of Parchman's retirement with an encore that pleased Blake Watkins, and one of the desk men had told her so when she'd called the office.

She had a career to think about, so she resolved to push thoughts of David aside and take care of business the rest of the week. There would be other races at other tracks. Perhaps a solution lay at one of those stops.

TRAFFIC WAS BUMPER to bumper on I-20, racing fans headed for a Sunday-long celebration at the monster speedway. "Race day at Talladega is like Mardi Gras," Herman Lanston had told her. "It's more than a sporting event—it's an *event*, period. It's impossible to explain it to anyone who hasn't seen it, just as it's impossible to explain the taste of lobster to anyone who hasn't eaten it."

She was beginning to understand what he meant. She thought she had left early and would beat the crowd, but the crowd had left early, too. Now she was moving ten feet and stopping, moving ten feet and stopping, locked in this procession of revelers.

Beth was sorry she had lowered the top of her red convertible. Her shining short blonde hair was a magnet for the fun-lovers. "Why don't you just drive that li'l ole car up here in the bed of this truck and help us drink some of this beer?" yelled a shirtless teenager who sprawled in a lawn chair on the back of a pickup. She buttoned the top button of her blouse when the grinning driver of a van in the adjacent lane said, "Need a co-pilot, hon?"

She drummed her fingers on the steering wheel and reflected on her first week on the racing beat. Despite being unnerved by the business with David, she had performed reasonably well. There was the memorable "scoop" on Parchman's retirement, the weak story about qualifying, an interesting feature on a driver whose hobby was painting, and a zinger in Sunday morning's paper on Arnie Shale and the trials and tribulations of a beginner in the big league. "Zinger" was the highest compliment Blake Watkins could pay, and that's what he called the story.

She had successfully avoided David, but a reporter couldn't cover stock car racing without covering David Marlow. Sooner or later she would have to approach him. The thought of interviewing David impersonally tore at the confidence her journalistic successes of the week had instilled.

Finally she reached the grounds of the speedway. It was October, but it was a hot Alabama sun that shone brilliantly on thousands of motor homes. Fans had stayed for several days, grilling steaks outside, playing softball, singing to the tunes of guitars around campfires at night. Now the race they had waited for was only three hours from starting.

Beth parked in the press lot behind the press box and walked through the grandstand to a gate that opened onto the track. It would be closed before the race started, but now it was open so that media members and others could take a final walk through the garage area. A security guard smiled when Beth showed him her credential.

She was careful walking down the steep bank of the track, and she knew fans were watching her, wondering why she had the clout to get into the garage.

Crews were pushing their cars into the starting slots on the pit road. A man yawned. Another winked at her. "Morning," she heard Pappy Draper say.

"Hi, Pappy," Beth said. "Is it going to be a good race?"

"They always are at Talladega," he said. "I think we'll be in the hunt. David feels confident."

"Great weather," she said, feeling foolish but not wanting to seem interested in how David felt.

"Uh, Beth . . ." he said tentatively.

"Yes, Pappy?"

"I mentioned to David that you didn't know Herman Lanston before this week."

"Yes?"

"I don't think he believed it."

"Well, why wouldn't . . ." She hushed. "Good luck, Pappy," she said, turning and walking away.

"Beth," he said.

She looked back. "What?"

"For whatever it's worth, I believe you."

She nodded. "I hope you win today."

Beth clenched her teeth and pretended to inspect a pile of tires. She was rubbing the raised letters on one of the fat black doughnuts when David said, "We'll use eighteen thousand dollars' worth of those today."

She turned and their eyes met. He wore an immaculate driving uniform that was snow white against his dark features, and the tingle—not unlike an electric shock—that always greeted the sight of him coursed through her neck and shoulders.

"Take care out there today," Beth said, not disguising her feelings for the man.

She read a strange wistfulness in his dark eyes and voice when he said, "I've never even been injured in a race car. I've seen friends get hurt, get killed, but the race always begins and ends for me like a regular work day for anyone else. I drive five hundred miles, then fly maybe five hundred more in my plane, and then I'm walking through the front door of my house at Daytona Beach. It all takes about eight hours, too."

He stared beyond her, momentarily lost in thought, as if evaluating his life. She pictured him, tired, turning the key to admit himself to a soundless house where no one welcomed him home. Then she saw a different scene, in which she was standing in the door, embracing him, and, finally, lying beside him in the darkness as the waves of the Atlantic broke in rhythm against the seawall at their threshold.

"Have you gotten good stories this week?" David asked, breaking the reveries in which they both were suspended. His tone was no more intimate than he might have used to pass the time with a stranger. It was as if he felt himself becoming familiar and immediately erected a defense.

"A couple, I guess," Beth answered. "The boss liked one on Arnie Shale that ran today."

"He's a good kid. Maybe he lets his foot overrule his brain occasionally."

"I remember another heavy-footed kid back on a dirt track near Tuscaloosa," Beth said.

"I did tear up a car or two. I've acquired a little judgment since then. People change."

"Yes, they surely do," Beth said.

"What is that supposed to mean?"

"You've certainly changed."

"I've changed? I'd say you've changed. About as much as anyone I've ever known."

She was confused, and it was a relief when a fat man wearing a cap with a Bibley Designs emblem slapped David on the back. "Mr. Bibley," David greeted him. "Beth, this is J. W. Bibley, president of the company that sponsors my car. Beth Barrett of *The Birmingham News*." They made small talk for a couple of minutes, Beth wished them luck, and she welcomed the opportunity to walk down the pit road.

She'd changed? David Marlow had the audacity to say she'd changed? He who had once held her tenderly in his arms, and who now was asking whether she had gotten good stories, as he might ask an awestruck sophomore intern whose name he didn't catch?

Well, at least he seemed to have reconciled himself to her continuing presence on the racing beat, that she would be at race after race, questioning him as the corps of reporters did each week, and he might as well make the best of it.

She stopped in front of Victory Lane, the destination that only one of the forty-three drivers would reach. It was a platform large enough to accommodate a car and those with an attachment to it. The floor was of black and white tile, symbolizing a checkered flag, and the track's logo was painted across the backdrop in slanted letters that were meant to convey an image of speed. It seemed curiously inappropriate that it was empty, that there was no activity. Beth thought of a movie theater without an image on the screen, without customers.

But moments after the end of the race the celebrants in a mini–Mardi Gras would swarm over Victory Lane. Beauty queens would kiss the winner, and so would his wife if he had a wife, and he would uncork a magnum of champagne and spray its contents on the scurrying cast. She hoped David would be the resident of Victory Lane for that magic moment, and for a second she pictured herself at his side, a miasma of champagne descending onto her blonde head.

"I'm already preparing my speech for the victory celebration," a voice said, and she smiled at the sight of Arnie Shale in a light blue uniform, the legs sharp with creases.

"Like it?" he asked. "I bought it this morning from Vern Parchman. He'd never even had it on. Lord knows, I couldn't afford it, but this is a special day."

"A special day?" Beth asked. "Why?"

"Well, of course I was kidding about the victory celebration. I ain't going to win today any more than I won last Sunday or the Sunday before that. But I'm going to show Herman Lanston something, and I've just got this intense feeling that today is really going to be the take-off point for my career."

She was puzzled. "Did you slip some jet fuel past the NASCAR inspectors?"

"Better'n that. I've got a hand grenade in my car."

"What in the world is a hand grenade? I've got a lot of learning to do on this beat."

"A hand grenade is a motor that is so strong it eventually will explode. That's the bad part. The good part is that it's strong enough to lead the race before it does."

"I'm still lost," Beth said. "Why would anyone want an engine like that?"

"Because when Herman Lanston goes to his motel tonight and pours himself a glass of Scotch and soda and replays the race in his mind, he's going to say, 'That dern li'l ole kid got up there in front and led for a few laps. He was ahead of Vern Parchman and David Marlow and the other stars. His engine blew, but by golly he was up there. I'll have to remember that next season when I go to choose a driver to replace Vern.'"

Now it was clear to her. At the party at the antebellum home, Lanston had advised Arnie Shale to impress him, and said that perhaps Arnie could drive his car. He hadn't meant it, but Arnie had acted on the statement.

"What happens when the engine blows?" Beth asked.

"Aw, you just drop down on the apron and coast around the track to the garage," Arnie said. "I'll probably shed a tear or two, thinking what the thing cost me.

"I left the party two minutes after Mr. Lanston told me he'd be watching me and called an engine builder in Michigan. I told him what I wanted, he put it together, and now it's in my car. And now I'm *sho' nuff* poor."

"What do you mean?"

"He wanted thirty grand for the thing. I had a little piece of land that my grandpaw left me, worth maybe forty. He took the deed."

"Oh, Arnie," Beth said. She wanted to explain that Herman Lanston wasn't interested in him, that he had wasted his money. But now the damage was done. She felt a jab of conscience. Should she have telephoned Arnie the night of the party and told him what Lanston said, that he wouldn't consider him as his driver? But, then, she had had no idea what the boy had in mind. She didn't even know anyone could build such an engine.

"Don't tell Mr. Lanston," Arnie said. "I wouldn't want him to know about all the special preparations. I'd just as soon he thought old Arnie's mechanical expertise and skill with a steering wheel took him to the front."

"Good luck, my friend," Beth said.

He stared at Victory Lane for a moment, and the slightest of smiles bent his cheek. He winked at Beth and started walking toward the garage. She watched him—a bowlegged bundle of bones and freckles and ambition, with no room for doubt. The racing beat was a good beat, she sighed to herself.

Wisps of smoke were rising from the infield, like scores of Indian signals. Those who chose not to sit in the stands had parked their vehicles—cars, trucks, campers, motor homes—inside the track, and there they would reside until long after the last racer's engine had gone quiet. They would barbecue steaks and hamburgers and hot dogs and drink beer and listen to the race on radios, because they could get only fleeting glimpses of cars as they roared by.

The frontstretch grandstand that stretched nine-tenths of a mile, and another stand that paralleled the backstretch, were being slowly populated. Many fans waited in the parking lots before taking their seats, they, too, washing down barbecue with beer and soft drinks. Even at this hour, long before the green flag waved, Beth was beginning to see what Herman Lanston had meant when he said the race wasn't just a sports event—it was an *event*.

The teams stocked their respective pits with tool boxes and air tanks and tires, even replacement windshields. She knew the crewmen, those sleight-of-hand artists in uniforms onto which were sewn the advertisements of their sponsors, could fuel a race car with twenty-two gallons of gasoline and change four tires in fourteen seconds. An hour remained before the flag-off of her first big stock car race, and she squeezed her hands in anticipation. No wonder Charlie Murphy hated to give up all this.

A gray-haired man, the chaplain of the racing fraternity, strolled toward a building in the infield, his flock in tow, growing as it passed each pit, like the following of the Pied Piper. Beth decided to listen to his service, so she fell in step.

The metal building shielded the drivers and crewmen and wives from the piercing Alabama sun. Beth peeked while the preacher prayed and she saw David staring at the floor, concentrating on his plea for the drivers' safety. David glanced at her and she smiled faintly, but he merely closed his eyes.

When the service ended, David disappeared into the restroom. Beth crossed the track and took her seat in the press box. It was tucked between decks of the grandstand. The distant mountains looked green and cool and quiet, a world apart from the scene that lay immediately before her.

Finally, the pre-race ceremonies ended, the barbecuers took their seats, and 170,000 fans joined in silence as the race's grand marshal, the president of an automotive accessory firm, dramatically intoned the words, "Gentlemen, start your engines!"

Chapter 6

*F*orty-three unmuffled motors came to life, their initial cries merely hinting at their power, and the multi-colored racers, each a rolling billboard, began to creep along the pit road, following the pace car to the scene of battle, the notorious high banks of Talladega Superspeedway.

The pit road emptied into the first turn, and the race cars slowly circled the mammoth track on the parade lap, their engines uttering oaths at the restraint. Beth's shoulders tingled as they passed the press box.

Two more laps and the pace car darted back onto pit road, and the drivers began to rev their motors, waiting for the appearance of the green flag that the flagman held out of sight behind his right hip.

Then he waved it, and the afternoon exploded in a riot of color and sound.

Vern Parchman immediately assumed the lead. David Marlow tucked the nose of his white Ford in behind Parchman's blue Chevrolet, scarcely a foot separating their cars. They leaped ahead of the field by perhaps twenty-five yards on the backstretch, but when the procession reached the frontstretch and the press box the others had caught up, and twenty cars were winding through the dogleg like a massive snake.

After five laps the twenty had separated themselves from the others, but they were tucked tight, nose to tail, one apparently as fast as the other.

"So that's the famous Talladega draft?" Beth asked the man sitting beside her, a friendly fellow from the hometown Talladega newspaper.

"That's it," he said. "They're able to run faster together than any could apart. With that wall of air ahead being broken up, slower cars are able to keep up in the vacuum."

Beth noticed that Arnie Shale was in the lead draft. In fact, he was in twelfth place. He had advanced thirteen positions in five laps.

When a big-name driver pulled out of line to pass, Arnie fell onto his bumper, and the duo sped by three men. "What's got into Shale?" the Talladega writer asked no one in particular. "He's got that thing honking today. He's running better than I've ever seen him."

Beth started to mention the susceptible engine, but she decided to play dumb to see if Arnie had told the other writer. "He doesn't usually drive so near the leader?" she asked.

"He hasn't got the equipment," the man said. "But, by gosh, look at him moving up there. He's challenging for fifth. That shade-tree operation has hit on the combination today."

The crowd was on its feet ten laps later when Arnie passed David Marlow for second place. Only Vern Parchman stood between him and the lead.

Beth wondered what Herman Lanston was thinking at this instant. Could he help but be impressed by what he was seeing? A driver who was practically unknown to most of the fans, who had no big money behind him, who had started in twenty-fifth place, had charged into second early in the afternoon, and he was challenging the champion for the lead.

She knew Lanston was sitting in one of the enclosed VIP lounges. He had told her he always rented one of the expensive buildings and entertained his salesmen and other business associates. While the fans sweated and drank beer, Lanston and his entourage ate roast beef and drank champagne and enjoyed the race in air-conditioned comfort. She decided to telephone him.

A soft-spoken man, obviously a servant, answered. A moment later Lanston was saying, "Yes?"

"I think you made an impression on Arnie Shale," Beth said, without identifying herself.

"Beth! And how are you liking your first race?" Lanston asked, ignoring what she had said.

"I love it. It's the most thrilling thing I've ever seen. Arnie is giving Vern a run for it, isn't he?"

Lanston laughed heartily. "Arnie is merely a temporary annoyance. Talladega is a car track, not a driver track. I mean it is so large and relatively easy to drive that the car becomes more important than the driver. Arnie has chosen to take advantage of that fact by somehow acquiring a powerful engine. It came from a firm in Michigan. It may blow on the next lap, it may blow fifty laps from now, but it can't last."

Beth was speechless. Lanston knew all about the hand grenade. He was no more impressed by Arnie today than he was that night at the mansion.

"Well, I'd like to see him have a high finish," she said. "He needs one."

"You don't *buy* victories in racing, Beth," Lanston said in the tone of a veteran counseling a neophyte, "but you do buy the chance at victory. Arnie simply doesn't have the money to buy a chance at victory. Even with that engine, what he will spend to run this race will be chump change compared to what we'll spend. Don't concern yourself with Shale. Prepare to watch a showdown between Vern Parchman and David Marlow."

"Goodbye, Herman," she said. "And good luck."

She felt like an idiot. She returned to her seat, and when Arnie passed Parchman for the lead moments later she couldn't share in the crowd's excitement.

She had known people like Herman Lanston, pragmatists who knew all the odds, dispassionate in the face of the facts. Her mother, the college history professor, was like that. "God is on the side that has the most artillery," she was fond of repeating. Beth was more comfortable with her father, the weekend golfer who believed he could hit a five-iron through an impossible thicket, and with Arnie Shale, who thought a hand grenade somehow could win him a ride in a competitive car.

And with David, who used to wring more out of his battered dirt-track racer than could have possibly been in it.

She watched as David passed Parchman for second. Parchman dropped to fifth, to seventh, to tenth. "Something's wrong with Vern's car," she said.

But the Talladega reporter shook his head. "He went up front and felt out the ones who want to lead. Now he's going to settle back and watch from the best seat in the house. He'll let them shoot each other down, then he'll be in the final game. Just like a basketball tournament."

"Does Arnie Shale have a chance to win?" she asked, hoping for a different answer than Lanston had spoken.

"Never say never, I always say," the reporter answered. "But I'll put it this way: if he won, it would be the biggest upset in stock car racing history. The hardscrabble teams like his can make a car run fast or they can make a car run long, but practically never can they make it run both fast and long."

Arnie and David Marlow were driving together at the head of the pack when both pitted for tires and gasoline. When they returned to the track, Beth was surprised to see David ahead of the younger driver by five hundred yards.

"The pit stops kill those teams, too," the man sitting beside her said. "These cars cover the length of a football field in a second, so every second lost in the pits translates into a hundred yards to be made up on the track."

But Arnie began running David down and after ten laps he caught him. In two more laps he passed David and resumed the lead.

Arnie led the hundredth lap of the 188-lap race, a success that provoked a spontaneous standing ovation from the crowd. Talladega was the track at which underdogs, men like James Hylton and Dick Brooks and Ron Bouchard, had won before—but never a dog so under as Arnie Shale.

Beth's emotions were as tangled as fishing lines in a storm. She wanted Arnie to win, for the shoe to fit Cinderella, for the hand grenade to miraculously hold together for eighty-eight more laps. But she wanted more for David to win, David who for some mysterious reason had welcomed her back into his life, then just as fervidly pushed her out of it. She loved him with that timeless love that binds one woman to one man, though every circumstance strives to loosen those ties. She wanted to break the cardinal press box rule of no cheering and urge David on to victory. Arnie Shale was the crowd's, but David was hers—or at least she vowed then and there that he would be hers again.

Another pit stop separated the cars, but again Arnie caught up. At 150 laps, he and David were a half-mile ahead of the field.

"Thirty-eight more times around," the Talladega reporter remarked. "I'd have bet my life that at this pace Arnie would have blown his motor, showered, and been halfway home by now. Wouldn't it be something if he managed to hold together and won this thing?"

The laps ticked off on the scoreboard, and with twenty to go the crowd rose to its feet to stay. The spectators thought they might be watching history, and they wanted to give it its due respect.

Twelve laps remained when it happened.

Arnie was leading David by fifty yards, and they were a mile ahead of Vern Parchman, who was in third place. White smoke began to belch from Arnie's car, and the rear wheels slid toward the outside of the track in the high-banked third turn. David darted to the inside, but Arnie's car shot inside, too, skiing on a pond of its own oil, and the nose of David's racer smashed into the driver's door of Arnie's machine with sickening force. Smoke poured from David's tires as the brakes attempted the impossible task of stopping a missile.

Arnie's car began flipping, turning sideways in a barrel roll. It climbed the bank of the turn and struck the outside retaining wall, and after a half-dozen rolls came to rest upside down in the infield. David's car, its steering mechanism sheared into uselessness, lumbered back up the bank and then, on four flat tires, slipped down for the final time.

Beth closed her eyes. She could not will herself to open them. Only the word, the horror of the word, forced them to see.

"*Fire!*"

The trained eye of the man next to her spotted the blaze, at first an orange flicker at the underside of David's car. Then it burst like a miniature atomic bomb.

Beth screamed, but at least she was not alone. The press box was a riot of yells and lamentations. Silence came only after a reporter watching through field glasses bellowed, "Marlow's out of the car. He climbed out by himself, and he's lying on the grass."

"Is he burned?" Beth demanded.

"Can't tell. The ambulance is blocking him from my view."

Beth darted from the press box and ran to her car, unaware and uncaring that Vern Parchman had taken the lead under the yellow caution flag. Her tires screamed and left black streaks as she left the parking lot and headed for the traffic tunnel that cut under the fourth turn of the speedway.

She sped to the infield hospital adjacent to the garage area, actually outrunning the ambulances that transported David and Arnie, ignoring the frantic gestures of a deputy sheriff. There were no parking places outside the hospital compound, so she left her car in the road and ran to the gate of the fence that sealed off the hospital from the public.

"Hey, you can't come in here," a security guard said, but she waved her press pass in this face and bounded by him just as the ambulances turned through the gate.

The sirens died and infield fans pressed against the fence, gawking as white-clad attendants flung open the back doors of the vehicles.

David gripped the sides of the stretcher as it was handed down, but his eyes were closed and there was no other sign he was alive. On his face was an inscrutable frown, as if he were more worried than injured. "David!" Beth said, but he did not open his eyes or change his expression. "David!"

Her breath came in gasps and the doctor glanced at her. "Better sit down," he said, but he walked away alongside David, and they disappeared into the small, square concrete building.

"Not so good," she heard a voice say. It was an ambulance attendant who was carrying one end of Arnie shale's stretcher. Another doctor nodded.

"My God," Beth said as she saw that the left side of the freckled, brown-haired youngster's face was crushed. "Is he alive?"

"He's alive," the ambulance driver said, lighting a cigarette. "I don't know for how long, through. That was a bad accident. Marlow got him right in the driver's door. Those are the worst ones. The rollbars can take a lot, but they can't always stand that. I remember one race here when . . . hey, the green flag's back out. Four laps to go. Looks like it's going to be between Vern Parchman and Speedy Minyard. Wanna stand up here on the back of the ambulance and watch the rest of it, honey?"

But Beth was walking beside the unconscious boy as the stretcher bearers reached the door of the hospital. "You can't come in here, Miss," a nurse said. The woman shook her head emphatically when Beth showed her press pass: "No good here."

Beth placed her forearm against the wall and rested her head on it. She closed her eyes and the lengthening shadows of the race track disappeared. She wished the sound would disappear, too. The roar of engines, exciting at first, now was a chilling accompaniment to horror, much as the guns of war.

"Parchman's gonna win it!" the ambulance driver shouted. "Minyard can't get around him!"

Beth heard the chorus of 170,000 throats as Vern Parchman crossed the finish line for a final time, a car length ahead of his nearest pursuer. "My God, David may be dying. Arnie may be dying. How can they care who wins?" Beth sobbed, but the attendant's eyes were riveted on the scene at the finish line, and he didn't hear her.

Chapter 7

*T*he race had been over for nearly an hour. Traffic moved out of the infield and through the tunnel at a glacial pace. Vern Parchman's fans still yelped his name, but they were more subdued now than they had been at the moment of victory. It had been a long day. They were tired, sunburned, and surfeited on barbecue and beer. "Wonder how Marlow and that kid are getting along," a rider on the bed of a pickup truck hollered to a rider on the bed of another pickup truck.

Beth wondered, too. She agonized. She wanted to knock on the hospital door, ask for a shred of information, a shred of hope, but she didn't want to distract any of the medical team that worked on David and Arnie inside.

The members of David's crew stood silently, hands in pockets, scuffing their toes in the gravel that covered the ground. Arnie Shale's crewmen were with them. The mechanics spoke in whispers that were lost even in the chirping of the birds that were settling in on the track to eat the scraps that fans had left.

"Think I'll bum a Coke from one of these fans," Pappy Draper said. "How 'bout one, Beth?"

"No, thanks," she said. He ambled out into the line of traffic and in seconds returned with a canned drink. Those were the first words they had spoken to each other, as if by refusing to acknowledge the accident, they somehow might hold it in abeyance.

The old man was tired. He should be working on passenger cars in his own shop in a nice, quiet small town, she thought. Then she chided herself for thinking it. He loved preparing fast cars for David; it was his life—and she knew Pappy wasn't thinking she should be home preparing dinner and helping kids with homework if she didn't choose to be.

Beth brushed a strand of hair off Pappy's forehead. "You're devoted to him, aren't you?" she said.

"He's like a son. I was his crew chief on the short tracks in Virginia. When he got his big break in the big league, he took me with him. He gave me a chance to play in that big league."

"Pappy," Beth said, "you saw that David was happy to see me here that first day. Then something happened. He hasn't been the same since. What is it?"

"I don't know," Pappy said. "I really don't. At first, he was just peeved about you being pals with Lanston. He pouted a little, like a fourteen-year-old who spots his sweetheart smiling at somebody else. You have to realize that his differences with Lanston are bone-deep. He'd rather have seen you with the Devil than with Herman Lanston. I know David as well as anybody does. There's a lot of little boy in him; it's part of his charm. I thought he'd be fine right away—but something else happened after that. Something hurt him deeply where you and Lanston are concerned. He wouldn't even talk to me about it."

Beth was dumbfounded. She knew, of course, that David was a kind, tender, caring man, and because he was, his feelings sometimes were as close to the surface as a boy's might be. As Pappy indicated, it was part of what made her love him. And she had correctly guessed that their problem was more complex.

The reporter from the Talladega paper appeared, along with several other men who had been in the press box. "Anything, Pappy?" he asked.

"Not yet," the crew chief said.

The hospital door opened and David Marlow walked out, into the fading sunlight. Beth fought to restrain herself from rushing to him, embracing him, kissing him in front of his crew and the other reporters.

The left sleeve of his driver's suit had been cut away and his arm was bandaged. Pappy patted him on the back and whispered something, and the disheveled driver nodded.

David glanced at Beth, but he didn't let his eyes linger. He looked toward the other reporters and said, "I'm okay. Just a concussion and a light burn on my arm here, no more than I usually get trying to fry bacon in the morning. Arnie's not so lucky. I guess the doc will tell you about him."

"Is Shale alive?" one man asked.

"He's alive," David said.

Beth realized just how right Charlie Murphy had been about covering racing. It was different. You miss a bunt, you lose a ballgame; you miss a corner, you lose your life. The "players" had to be tougher than football players. And those who covered racing had to be tough, too. She hoped she was up to it. She felt as helpless as if she were covering a presidential news conference. She should be comforting the man she loved instead of being one of the interrogators.

"Describe what happened," the writer from the Talladega paper said.

"Well, as you saw, Arnie Shale was running the greatest race of his life. I was shocked his equipment had lasted as long as it had, and I didn't feel so comfortable running on his tail. But I was afraid to let him get too far ahead, too."

"Parchman wasn't," somebody said.

David frowned. "I'm not Vern Parchman. He runs his style, I run mine. He has won a lot of races, but so have I." Beth saw that fire had replaced the tiredness in his eyes.

"Go on," a writer said.

"I saw a little puff of smoke come out of Arnie's exhaust, and I knew what was happening. In a split second there was a big puff of smoke, his engine blew, and it dumped oil on the track.

"His rear wheels got in his own oil, and his car spun. I had nowhere to go, and I tagged him right in the driver's door. My face shield hit the rollbar, and I blanked out momentarily. Evidently a piece of debris from his car cut my oil line, the oil hit something hot on my car and caught fire. The fire probably looked worse from the stands than it really was.

"By the time my car stopped, I was aware of what was happening. I loosened my harness and plopped out the window. My arm got in some burning grass for a moment, but I'm fine. I'll be ready for the next race."

"Could you have beaten Shale if his engine hadn't blown?"

"His car was a little faster, but I think my experience might have gotten me around him at the end. But we'll never know that, will we?

"I'll say one thing, and I hope you quote me. Any car owner looking for a young driver with a lot of promise could do a lot worse than hiring Arnie Shale."

"If he lives," a TV reporter said.

David frowned and nodded.

He had never looked her way after that first glance. Beth was dejected. She had been aching inside while he was in the hospital, and he hadn't even acknowledged her presence. Now he was walking away, accepting a drink of Pappy Draper's Coke.

"David," Beth said.

He turned and faced her, frowning. "Yes'um?"

"What's wrong?"

"What's wrong? Well, we just lost a pretty expensive race car, for openers."

Her eyes flashed. "You know what I mean. What's happened between us?"

He sighed and gazed at her a moment before he spoke, "Beth, there's a kid lying in there who is broken in body, and financially, and maybe in spirit. Herman Lanston is responsible. He plays with people's lives and doesn't give a damn when his toy breaks because he'll just get another one. Arnie Shale isn't the first person he's ruined.

"He tells a naive kid to perform like a daredevil on the track and maybe he'll get a shot at driving for him, when he knows damn well he wouldn't let the boy through the front door of his racing shop. You and Lanston must have had a big laugh about it after the party."

"Now, just a minute," Beth interrupted. "I didn't . . ."

"Now the kid looks like a train has hit him, and Lanston's up there in his VIP box where he and his pals are polishing off the last morsels of a feast that cost more than Arnie Shale's share of today's purse. In a few minutes he'll board his helicopter and it will lift him over the traffic to the airport where his jet waits. Arnie will catch a helicopter, too, but it will be the one that transports injured drivers to a Birmingham hospital. And Lanston won't even inquire about Arnie."

"David, I had no idea anything like this could possibly happen," Beth said, exasperated. "I don't know enough about racing to expect . . ."

"Miss Barrett!"

She turned to see a member of the speedway public relations staff fumbling for his credential to show a security guard. Finally, the tired old man in the dark blue uniform was satisfied and motioned him through the gate into the hospital compound.

"Your sports editor called the press box," he said breathlessly. "Wanted to speak to you. Said he wanted to tell you to file a quick story for the first edition, then beat it down here to the infield hospital and do a rewrite, featuring the Arnie Shale angle. Since he's a Springville boy, that's the big story today, he said. I had to tell him I couldn't find you, and he sounded plenty mad. I waded through the crowd down here to try to keep you from getting in trouble."

"The Arnie Shale angle," David said, smirking. "You should be able to do that one up brown."

Beth looked at her watch and gasped. "I'm missing my first-edition deadline because I came here to see about you," she said.

David's look softened. "I'm sorry," he said. "Better get on it." He turned and walked to a waiting passenger car.

Beth ran across the track and through the gate that had been open before the race. She scurried up the steps of the press box to her seat and telephoned Blake Watkins.

"Blake! Sorry, but I rushed to the infield hospital to do the Arnie Shale angle immediately, and I let the time slip up on me," she said lamely. "I guess we missed the first edition, huh?"

"No, Miss Barrett, we didn't miss the first edition," he said with acid in his voice. "*You* missed the first edition. We have a bare-bones story that Charlie Murphy wrote for us in ten minutes. Thank God when he left the paper he became a racing flack. When no one could find our Wonder Woman I got one of the PR men here to dig Charlie out of a VIP lounge. He was about half snockered, but that never kept Charlie from making complete sentences, and it didn't today."

She was stunned. "Charlie Murphy wrote my story?"

"Hell, no. No one wrote your story. Your story isn't written yet. Charlie was glad to help us in a pinch."

"I bet he was." Beth sighed.

Watkins was silent for a moment; then, his voice firm but no longer angry, he said, "Beth, look, I know why you rushed to the infield hospital and missed your deadline. I can sympathize with it. But that doesn't excuse it. Maybe I made a mistake putting you on the racing beat, since you and David Marlow used to be . . . well."

"I can handle it, Blake," she said. "I'm sorry about today. I can handle it. I'll get on that second-edition story right now, hitting the Arnie Shale angle hard."

She hung up. And wondered if she could handle it.

Chapter 8

A man who claimed to have invented a wondrous new system of stretching exercises for women marathon runners was in Birmingham, begging for publicity, and when Blake Watkins got him off the telephone, the sports editor tossed his indecipherable notes on Beth's desk.

"He'll be in the coffee shop at the Sheraton at noon," Watkins told her. "Might be a good feature in this."

Dwight MacMillan, a rookie sports writer with a mild crush on Beth, grinned as Watkins walked away. "Any way I can get an advance copy of your story?" he asked her. "It sounds so interesting that I don't think I can wait until it comes out in the paper."

She knew Watkins was punishing her for her failure at the race two days before. He was assigning her to write what those in the business call a non-story. It would merely take up space, say nothing, and go unread except by an infinitesimal percentage of subscribers.

"Maybe I can write a book about it," Beth told MacMillan. "It would be a best-seller and I'd get rich. Then you and I could run off to a South Seas island and live snappily ever after."

"The first woman I ever kissed was an older woman," he said. "Her name was Mamma."

"Well, you've done a lot of growing up in the twenty years since. Maybe even ten years' worth."

Beth walked the dozen or so blocks to the Sheraton. The punishing Alabama summer was fading into autumn, and a playful October breeze was invigorating.

She would phone Carraway Methodist Medical Center when she finished with the marathon man. Arnie Shale had been helicoptered to the Birmingham hospital from the infield care center at Talladega Superspeedway, and it was issuing reports on his condition three times a day.

This was Tuesday, two days after the race, and Arnie hadn't regained consciousness, but the morning report said his doctors were "cautiously optimistic" about his condition. She seized on the term as a positive sign, refusing to allow herself to reflect on its essential meaninglessness. He had suffered a head injury and assorted fractures of the cheek, arm, leg, ribs, and sternum.

Beth had gone to the hospital on Monday, but she had been told no one but Arnie's family could see him. His parents and his older brother sat in the intensive care waiting room, their expressions the familiar flat-blank look that could be found on thousands of faces in thousands of hospitals. They had been there all night, catching winks of sleep when they could.

They were country folks. Both the men wore jeans and plaid shirts, and in their laps were identical baseball-style caps with emblems that read *Shale Auto Repairs, Springville, Ala.* Arnie's mother was plain, her shoulder-length hair straight and lifeless. Beth guessed she, like her husband, was approaching fifty. She, too, wore jeans. The red letters on her white tee shirt bespoke her love for the Alabama Crimson Tide. One of the biggest NASCAR races of the year had just been contested, but in this state a huge majority of residents was more concerned with the fate of Alabama's and Auburn's football teams.

Beth introduced herself to the Shales and offered condolences for

Arnie's misfortune. The men didn't speak. The woman nodded and said, "Thank you."

Beth wondered if they had read the feature story she had written about Arnie. It might form some link between her and the Shales, and perhaps they would talk to her.

"We read it," the woman said. And that's all she said.

Beth was embarrassed. "Were you at the race?" she asked.

"His daddy and his brother were watching on TV," Mrs. Shale said. "I was reading my Bible. They encourage Arnie, but I hate this racing. I don't watch it. I didn't watch it when he was racing at the fairgrounds in Birmingham. If it wasn't for this racing, my boy wouldn't be in this hospital. Yes, I read your story, and it made me sick, for I knew it would just encourage Arnie more.

"And I'm not telling you this to put in your paper. It's—how do you newspaper folks say it?—off the record. No comment."

Beth turned to the men. They stared straight ahead, at a wall. What could they say? Arnie might, indeed, die because he did something his mother begged him not to do. It was no time for a philosophical discussion of an adult's right to choose his own course.

Arnie bucked the odds to be a racer, led a hardscrabble life, actually sleeping in a tent at the campgrounds at some speedways. She could only imagine how much more trying it was for him because of the division it caused in his family. But she could understand his mother's viewpoint, too. Could she, Beth, be enthusiastic and supportive if she had a daredevil son? Maybe not.

"I'm sorry," Beth told the Shales. She was relieved to step into the hospital parking deck and drive her car down the ramps and onto the streets that led back to her office at the *News.*

"I met Arnie Shale's family at the hospital," she told Blake Watkins before he could ask, "but they wouldn't talk to me."

"They didn't say anything?" Blake asked, emphasizing the last word.

"Nothing. Just that they didn't want to talk to a newspaper reporter."

That had been Monday. Now, a day after meeting the Shales, she was meeting a guy who invented stretching exercises for female marathoners.

She walked into the coffee shop and, though it was busy, she knew she had spotted her man. He was skinny, with the gaunt face and undernourished look of so many running enthusiasts. He spread a phony smile across his face, waved at her, stood, and pulled a chair out for her. Anatomical drawings were spread all over the table.

She remembered what Charlie Murphy had said, that he couldn't stand to leave stock car racing for baseball, that he'd be asleep in three innings. She had covered just one race, had her emotions twisted and torn, but already she wished it were time for the next event on the circuit. A story on stretching exercises, indeed.

BETH LOWERED THE TOP on her roadster and began the 450-mile trip to that next event, a four-hundred-miler at Rockingham, North Carolina. It was chilly with the top down, but it was liberating, so she wore a denim jacket and toboggan and brought along a Thermos of hot coffee.

Forty miles into her trip, cruising on I-20, she saw Talladega Superspeedway. A few days before, it had been overrun with people and crackling with excitement; now its grandstands were empty and the only activity was that of the crews that cleaned up the massive stadium after a race, hauling away tons of cans, bottles, and other refuse. She was past it in a moment, and then it disappeared from her rear-view mirror.

She thought David Marlow must be traveling to Rockingham, too. She pictured him piloting his plane through the clouds. She imagined the view the Atlantic Ocean and the coastline must present as he became airborne at Daytona Beach.

She pictured herself sitting beside him as he pointed out the sights. She would nuzzle against his neck and he would laugh and warn,

"You're going to put us into the sea." But she wouldn't stop, because she knew he didn't want her to. Finally he would say, "I'm glad you came back into my life. I love you."

But that wasn't reality. Reality was that she was traveling alone, and the only warmth was coming from a cup of coffee. What had happened to change their relationship? David was delighted to suddenly discover her on his turf, Talladega Superspeedway. That was evident. But, just as suddenly, he treated her as if she were merely another reporter. No, not even that well; he treated her with disdain.

She was determined to learn the truth. Before she returned home from Rockingham she would have the facts, as a good reporter should—even if it was a matter of the heart instead of a story. She promised herself that.

She reached Rockingham after dark, grabbed a hamburger at a fast-food joint, and settled into her motel. She shared a nightcap of bourbon and water with a Charlotte racing writer beside the pool, turned in early, and slept well, tired from the drive. She loved her little Miata, but it wasn't built for long trips.

The next day she reported for duty at North Carolina Speedway. It measured a little more than a mile around. It seemed a toy to eyes that had been on the 2.66-mile Talladega Superspeedway for several days.

Beth went directly to David Marlow's stall in the garage. He hadn't arrived, but Pappy Draper and his mechanics were honing the white Ford that David would drive in Sunday's race. The hood was up and two heads had disappeared into the engine compartment. Three sets of legs protruded from underneath the car.

She wondered if Pappy would even remember her name, but as she started to reintroduce herself he grinned and said, "Beth! I'm glad to see you! How was your trip? Did you drive or fly?"

She decided to get to the point immediately. "Pappy, can I talk to you?" she asked.

"Sure."

She shamelessly turned on the charm, taking his arm and walking him away from the car. "I've got a problem," she said. What old codger could resist helping a pretty young woman solve her problem?

"David and I were, well, close at one time. It was wonderful seeing him again at Talladega. I know he was pleased to see me, too. But, then—to use a racing term—our reunion hit the wall. I don't know why. It had something to do with Herman Lanston. I wish you would find out and tell me what happened." She squeezed his arm, a sign that she was depending on him.

Pappy Draper melted. "I'll do my damnedest to find out," he promised. "I'm having lunch with David today at some civic club he's speaking to. I'll try to pin him down."

"Thanks."

She strolled through the garage area, speaking to drivers she had met at Talladega. "How are you?" Vern Parchman said. Obviously, he didn't even remember the name of the reporter to whom he had given a scoop, the story of his impending retirement.

She spotted Herman Lanston talking to an official at the NASCAR trailer. He didn't see her. Good.

"Hey, Bama Belle, how's Arnie Shale?" a crewman asked, remembering her from Talladega.

"They think there's a good chance he will live," she said, "but he isn't out of the woods yet."

"Brad Statham had the same thing happen to him a few years ago," the crewman said. "He might give you a good story."

She liked these racing people. They were down-to-earth, unpretentious. "That's a good idea," she said, and she meant it. It was a very good idea. It would be a timely, related feature for tomorrow's paper.

She went to Brad Statham's garage stall and found the driver spreading a slice of bread with mustard, crafting a baloney sandwich on a workbench. She introduced herself and said she'd like to interview him when he got time.

"I've got time now," he said. "How about a sandwich?"

So they ate baloney sandwiches and drank soft drinks, and Beth listened as Statham compared what happened to him years before with what happened to Arnie Shale days before.

"I was running third with twelve laps to go in the five-hundred-miler at Daytona, gaining a second a lap," he said. "I had consistently outrun both the cars ahead of me, but I had fallen back on pit stops. We had made our last pit stop, though, and I'm sure I would have passed them and won the race.

"But, as they say, it ain't over till the checkered flag falls. Three cars that were two laps down were fighting for position, and they tangled and spun. There was nowhere for me to go. I got caught up in the melee. I woke up a week later in the hospital at Daytona."

He shook his head. "Hell of a way to milk an extra week out of a Florida vacation, wasn't it?"

Beth laughed and underlined the quote after she jotted it down in her notebook. She'd use that one, for sure.

"What I'm about to tell you now is off the record, okay?" Statham said. Beth nodded, but he insisted: "Say it."

"It's off the record," she assured him.

"Herman Lanston was so disappointed that he never even came to see me in the hospital or after I got home. For the first time he was going to win the Super Bowl of stock car racing, but then it slipped away. They said he was already walking toward Victory Lane.

"I recuperated and could have driven the final half of the season, but Lanston released me. He said it was my fault. Obviously, it wasn't. Every TV angle showed I was the helpless victim, but he lawyered me and, rather than get into a long, drawn-out legal battle, I agreed to a small settlement."

"Herman Lanston?" Beth said. "He owned your car?"

"Yep. I was one of his early drivers. We won two races and finished fourth in the point standings the season before. I think we would have been a force in racing for years to come, but he held that wreck against me then and always has. Not only did he fire me, he's blocked some deals that I could have gotten, like endorsements and sponsorships. My career has never been any more than mediocre since then."

Beth was stunned. Was the man Brad Statham was describing the same man who was so courtly and helpful to her?

"Then why is what you told me off the record?" she asked. "Here's a chance to let the public know you were treated unfairly."

"Uh uh," Statham said emphatically. "The last thing I need is to get into a battle with Herman Lanston in the newspapers or anywhere else. He'd cut my throat and drink my blood before I knew what happened."

Their conversation went back on the record, and Statham described his comeback and wished Arnie Shale well. Beth could hardly formulate her questions, for thinking about Herman Lanston.

She went to the press room and wrote her story. She'd tack some notes on the bottom of it at the end of the day, and perhaps Blake Watkins would praise her foresight in interviewing Brad Statham.

When she finished, she saw David Marlow and Pappy Draper in deep discussion. Practice would begin in a few minutes, and Draper was telling Marlow whatever crew chiefs tell drivers when practice is a few minutes away.

She waited until David had driven onto the track before she approached Draper. Pappy handed his stopwatch to a crewman and told him to time David's laps. "Come with me," he told Beth, steering her into the drivers' lounge.

She sat on a sofa and he perched on the edge of a chair. "Here's what happened," Draper said. "Charlie Murphy, your old buddy from the newspaper, sabotaged you. He told David you were one of Lanston's girls."

"What? I had never met Lanston before last week. I had never even heard of him, unless I had read his name on a can of beans." Beth wasn't one to use profanity, but she added, "That son of a bitch Murphy."

"I believe you," Draper said. "Everybody in racing knows Charlie Murphy, but not everybody likes him. He has stabbed a driver or two in the back along the way. One fellow complained about Charlie's misquoting him, so Charlie dug and dug until he found a charge against the guy for drunk driving and leaving the scene of an accident. It happened when he was just a kid, but Charlie wrote about it, and the fellow lost his sponsor."

"Surely David didn't believe Charlie," Beth said. "About me, I mean."

"I'm afraid he did," Draper answered. "Sometimes the way to be believed is to tell a big lie, not a little one or a middle-sized one. Look the fellow in the eye and tell it. Make it big enough that he'll think no one would make up something like that."

"Charlie told David that you shacked up with Lanston every Talladega race week. Said he sent his plane for you at other times. Said this had been going on for a few years."

"That sorry son of a bitch," Beth said, emphasizing the adjective.

Draper sighed. "That ain't all. He told David that Lanston used his influence to get him taken off the racing beat and you put on it. Said Lanston Farms canned goods are big on the shelves of grocery stores that advertise with your paper, and that Lanston used that to sway the paper. Said with you on the racing beat, y'all could be with each other regularly."

Beth took a deep breath and tried to regain her composure. "No doubt Charlie was embarrassed by being replaced by a woman," she said. "This is his way of explaining it. To David, and, probably, half the people in this garage. It not only slanders me, it slanders Herman Lanston. All I did was go to a party with a widower."

"Widower?" Draper said. "Is that what Lanston told you? He's not a widower. He's very much married. She's his third wife, but he and the present Mrs. Lanston have been hitched, oh, I guess twelve years or more. She doesn't come to races. Looks down her nose at the racing folks. But I met her at the NASCAR banquet in New York. I guess the grand ballroom of the Waldorf wasn't beneath her."

Beth and Pappy walked out of the drivers' lounge into bright sunshine, and she shaded her eyes. David Marlow spotted them immediately. He frowned and impatiently summoned Draper with a motion of his hand. Pappy double-timed to the garage stall, and Beth followed.

"It's too loose, Pappy," David said, ignoring Beth's presence. "Where have you been? You need to get this piece of junk fixed. We don't have all day."

She saw Pappy's eyes narrow. "We've been together a long time, David," he said, "and that's the first time you've ever called one of my cars a piece of junk. Maybe we should just sell it to a junkyard and skip this race."

Beth considered keeping her mouth shut. She really did. But so what if this was a bad time to speak up? When would be a good time? She stepped forward, punched David's chest with her forefinger, and said quite loudly, "Speaking of junk, Mr. Marlow, that lying Charlie Murphy has been feeding you plenty of junk about Herman Lanston and me, and I'm tired of it. I had never laid eyes on Lanston until last week at Talladega. Charlie is teed off at me because they took him off the racing beat and put me on it, and he's making up lies as he goes."

She was embarrassed when she saw that the crewmen of three cars, including David's, had stopped their work to listen to the crazy woman dressing down the racing star.

Marlow was too startled to answer at first, but then he said, "I've known Charlie Murphy for years, and I've never . . ."

"David, David, David!" Pappy interrupted, like a school teacher scolding a pupil. "She's right. She didn't know Herman Lanston from Herman Munster. Murphy made it up."

David's expression was one of profound confusion. "How do you know?" he asked Pappy.

"You've always said I was the best judge of people you've ever known, haven't you? Well, that's how I know."

David took Beth's hands in his. "I didn't want to believe it," he said in the soft voice that she used to hear when they would take long walks at night by Denny Chimes on the University of Alabama campus. "It wasn't something the girl I used to know would have done. But people change, and I hadn't seen you in years."

"It's not something the girl you know now would do, either," she said.

"I believe you." His words floated on a sigh of relief.

David reached out to embrace her, but the voice of the NASCAR official blared from the loudspeaker. "Rain's a few minutes away from the speedway. If you want practice laps, you'd better get them in a hurry."

"We'll talk later," David said, squeezing her shoulders. He took his helmet from the roof of the car and climbed inside.

She bestowed the embrace that would have been David's on his crew chief instead. "Thanks, Pappy," she said.

He blushed and nodded and pretended to be sorting through some tools in a box as a couple of his crewmen bleated, "Awright, Pappy D.!"

Chapter 9

Driving a race car two hundred miles an hour in combat with forty-two other drivers is not something that a sane person would do, David had told the members of the Rockingham Kiwanis Club at their luncheon meeting.

He always began his speeches with that line. It wasn't true, of course, but it provoked a laugh. Then he would add, "If you don't understand why I do this, no explanation will suffice; if you do understand why I do this, no explanation is necessary."

He understood perfectly why he did it. He couldn't live without racing, without turning left on green. It was an addiction, an obsession—and he didn't mind if some columnist used those words, despite their negative connotations.

From the first time he drove a friend's hobby car at a quarter-mile bullring, David knew he would be a racer. If he could make the big time, that would be wonderful; if he couldn't make the big time, he would work at a regular job and drive on the short tracks. But *not* racing was out of the question. He'd returned to his home in the tiny community of Wellington, Alabama, that night, assured that he had found his life's calling. He was sixteen years old.

"How can you not be afraid?" a newspaper or television interviewer inevitably would ask. "You know as well as anyone better than most—what can happen."

"All I can tell you is that I'm not afraid. I don't know why I'm not. I never get in a race car thinking I might be killed or injured. That never crosses my mind."

AND HE DID know better than most what can happen, for his younger brother Pete had lost his life in a racing crash.

"I don't mind talking about it," he told Beth as they ate Italian food and drank a good Chianti. He remembered that Italian was her favorite food when she was a college student and he was a dirt-tracker, and after Pappy's revelation of Charlie Murphy's duplicity had restored his trust in her, he'd asked her out. The man who owned the restaurant was proud to have David as a customer when the tour stopped in Rockingham, and he provided them with a small private dining room, away from the fans who inevitably turned David's attempt to eat a quiet meal into an autograph session.

David refilled Beth's wine glass and said, "When I tell you this, you will understand why I despise Herman Lanston."

He gazed out the window, watching the lights of vehicles and businesses doing a kaleidoscopic dance on the rain-spattered street, chose his words, and said, "Four years ago I drove for Lanston. We were leading in the championship points standings, and I think we would have won the title.

"Everything at his racing compound was first class. He spared no expense. If he wanted a crew member from another team, he would offer him a huge increase in pay and hire him away. Our cars, our equipment, everything, were the best money could buy.

"But that wasn't enough for Lanston. He didn't want a mere sporting chance at the championship; he wanted a guarantee. He constructed a mysterious building on the compound grounds. I say mysterious because not everyone was allowed inside. Even I wasn't, and I was the driver.

Only three members of the crew were admitted. I saw strangers enter and leave the building.

"'Don't worry about it,' Lanston would answer when I asked about the building. Then one day he told me he wanted me to come with him. We entered the building, and there were four Lanston Farms cars, brand new. Seven men in immaculate white smocks stood beside the cars. They looked like laboratory workers, not mechanics. And, in a sense, they were working in a laboratory.

"Lanston said, 'This is David Marlow,' which they already knew, of course. He said. 'You don't need to know these gentlemen's names, David. Just look on them as friends who will deliver us the championship.'"

Beth's curiosity was boiling. "Who were they?" she asked.

David smiled at her eagerness. "They were engineers," he said. "Or at least that's what Lanston called them. I'm not sure who they were.

"Lanston explained to me that they had created the ultimate cheater cars, and . . ."

Beth was on the edge of her chair. "What's a cheater car?" she asked.

"I forgot you're new to racing," David said. "I'll give you a history lesson.

"Cheating used to be a way of life for NASCAR mechanics. By cheating, I mean circumventing the car specifications. Typical methods involved hiding fuel so the racer could go father between pit stops, lowering the car so it would hug the track better, using a squirt of nitrous oxide gas to give the car a sudden burst of speed, losing weight . . ."

Beth smiled. "Explain the part about losing weight," she said. "If I eat much more of this lasagna I'll need to know how they do that."

"Some hid BBs in the car so it safely made the minimum weight in pre-race inspection," he said. "Then they turned the BBs loose during the race. The guys behind didn't particularly appreciate a barrage of air-rifle shot, but there wasn't much they could do about it. Some used water for the same purpose. The driver would flip a lever and water would come pouring out onto the track. Presto, a lighter car.

"This kind of stuff was more or less considered part of the game in the early days. An old NASCAR official referred to it as 'creative engineering' and admitted that he admired the ability of the mechanical geniuses who could slip something by his inspectors.

"One crew chief made the minimum weight by filling the tires with water. Another inserted wooden blocks in the springs so the car would meet height specifications—and when it hit a bump on the track the blocks would fall out and the car would be lower. One car builder created a racer that was seven-eighths scale. It was perfect to the eye, but as illegal as a bank robbery.

"The most famous cheating story involved Smokey Yunick, the mechanical genius who had a garage across town from the track in Daytona Beach. NASCAR was giving Smokey a tough time in inspection at Daytona International Speedway, and finally the inspectors made him remove the fuel tank from his car. Smokey got tired of the hassle, so he got in the car and drove it out of the speedway and all the way to his garage across town—without a fuel tank.

"Smokey said that's just a story, that it isn't true, but the point is those guys were so adept at creative engineering that a lot of people believe it could have happened.

"The cheating story to end all cheating stories goes back to the old days when they raced on a course that included a stretch of public highway and the hard-packed sands of the beach.

"A driver built two identical race cars. He hid one in the garage of a house on the backstretch—the highway—and a henchman, anonymous in helmet and goggles, subbed for him at the starting line on the beach.

"When the race started, the hidden car rolled out of the garage and onto the course, half a lap ahead of the field. The original starting car dropped back in the pack immediately, and when it reached the backstretch it pulled into the garage. Needless to say, the fellow who cooked up that scheme won the race."

Beth waited for David to laugh and tell her the last anecdote wasn't really true. But he didn't, and her curiosity about racing perked, like coffee bubbling into a pot. It was fascinating. Maybe Charlie Murphy was right; maybe it was the *only* sport.

"All right, fast-forward to more modern times," David said. "Lanston told me his engineers had built cars that shredded the NASCAR rule book. The rules had been broken before, he said, but the difference was that, one, they'd never been broken on such a comprehensive, all-inclusive scale in any one car, and, two, NASCAR could never detect these violations because the violators were too skilled to be caught.

"The guy spoke with pride, as if he'd commissioned a great artist to paint a masterpiece or a supreme composer to write a magnificent work of classical music. He had, in effect, committed the ultimate racing crime.

"The violations were in the motor, in the aerodynamics, in the fuel capacity, in the chemistry of the fuel itself, even in the tires, which had been treated with a chemical that increased speed. The engineers and three key members of the crew had pooled their knowledge to create them."

David smiled bitterly and shook his head, and the inch-long scar on his cheek danced. Attractively, Beth thought.

"Lanston had all the bases covered—he believed. What he didn't count on was what happened next. He asked me what I thought about his scheme and I said, 'Herman, I won't drive these cars.'

"I honestly don't think it had ever occurred to him that I'd be anything but excited and grateful to him for figuring a way for us to steal the championship.

"He laughed, like he knew I was kidding, even winked at one of the engineers, and told me, 'You won't have to drive these babies. They'll practically drive themselves.'

"I said, 'I mean it, Herman, I won't do this.' The expression I saw on his face then was one of pure hatred. I'm not exaggerating; he hated me. Instantly."

Beth waved off David's offer to pour her another glass of wine. "I'm not sure I understand," she said. "I thought you just said skirting the rules was part of the game, that it was called creative engineering."

"I said it used to be that way," David corrected her. "In fact, the philosophy was a cliché: 'A cheater doesn't always win, but a winner always cheats.' Stock car racing used to be a down-home slice of Americana, and the cheating stories were part of its folklore, but it's a huge, mainstream sport now. Every race is nationally televised. Huge corporations sponsor racing teams. It's not just a bunch of good ole boys partying all night and driving all day for a ham and a bottle of wine. Times have changed. Racing doesn't need cheating scandals any more than baseball, basketball, or football does. Plus, I simply didn't want to win races and championships that way."

"A ham and a bottle of wine?"

"That's an ancient racing story. Old Buck Baker said he won a race one time and the winner's purse was a ham and a bottle. When he opened it, it wasn't even whiskey; it was wine."

And probably not as good as this wine, Beth thought, as she decided to have one more glass after all. Her companion was a handsome, interesting man, the food was excellent, the night was mellow, and the stories were lively. So what if she was feeling a little lightheaded. "What happened after you refused to drive?" she asked.

"Lanston said we had a contract, that I was legally obligated to drive for him the rest of the season, and that if I didn't he would sue me. I knew he was bluffing, of course. The last thing Lanston Farms needed was me testifying in court about his cheater cars.

"I gave him a day to cool off and asked him to reconsider his decision to use those cars, but he said the cars would race and if I wasn't in the driver's seat, someone else would be.

"I'll give Herman credit. He built a great racing team by not standing pat. He was always trying to improve things, even when we were winning. His favorite saying was, 'If it ain't broke, fix it anyway.' And he considered his cheater cars as simply an extension of that philosophy.

"I pointed out that it was the middle of the season, and all the top drivers had rides—that he and the team would be better off with me driving legal cars than with some lesser driver in the cheater cars. I told him he was throwing the championship away by changing drivers in midstream. After all, it's a driver's championship, and the points we'd accumulated went with me.

"But arguing with Herman Lanston is like arguing with a mountain. It won't move, no matter how logical your point is. So that was the end of Herman Lanston's and David Marlow's relationship. Pappy walked, too."

Beth knew she was sitting across the table from a special person, a man who wouldn't sacrifice his integrity for money or a championship, who knew his sport deserved better than the manipulation of Herman Lanston. She studied his dark visage, his dark eyes, his hair as black as the night, the little scar on his cheek, an emblem of a life lived on the edge. "So what happened then?" she asked.

"Well, as you can imagine, our split-up was big news on the sports page. All I ever told the media was that I'd decided to go fishing for the rest of the season. 'Why?' they demanded. 'I enjoy fishing,' I told them. 'Don't you enjoy fishing? I thought everybody liked to fish.' Lanston issued a terse statement that we had parted company, and he would soon announce the identify of the man who would drive for him the rest of the season. He gave no reason for the split. The media was totally frustrated, and none of them ever learned the true story—and I'm trusting you now that you won't write it. Somebody called our split 'the stock car racing mystery of the ages.'

"The next event was the July race at Daytona Beach, and one of my old crewmen tipped me off that Herman was going to offer the ride to my brother Pete. At first it made no sense to me, but then I figured it out. I wouldn't squeal about the rules violations if Pete were driving the car, and if Pete made a good showing that would further rub it in as far as I was concerned. Of course, I wouldn't have squealed anyway. I believed him when he said inspectors couldn't find the alterations, and if I had squealed I would have been accused of sour grapes at best, and sued for slander at worst."

David sighed, gazed out the window, and Beth caught a barely perceptive shaking of his head, as if denial could somehow change the facts.

"Pete and I weren't on very good terms anyway," David said. "Lanston knew that, and it made it even more satisfying for him. Pete was impulsive, on and off the track. I was ten years older and experienced, and I had tried to advise him, but he resented it. I told him repeatedly to drive with his head as much as with his right foot, but he thought all a driver needed was to be bolder than everyone else. Then he'd wreck and his car would be destroyed, and he'd be angry at me because it happened the way I warned him it would. I told him to not accept a certain sponsorship, but he did anyway, and then the money never came, and he was left holding the bag.

"So when I told him not to get involved with Herman Lanston, he said I was jealous, that instead of encouraging him in his racing career, all I'd ever said was don't, don't, don't. Just because I'd blown off the best ride on the circuit, that didn't mean he should turn it down. He said a driver's job was to drive the car, not pass judgment on how the crewmen—or imported engineers—had done their job.

"I told Pete he simply didn't have the experience to drive that car. He was just twenty years old. He had competed on the bullrings three years and had a grand total of two races on superspeedways, one at Daytona and one at Talladega, both with an ARCA owner who was trying to trade on my name. The guy thought having David Marlow's brother as his driver would lure a sponsor, but it didn't work. Pete was a lost ball in high weeds in both those races. He crashed and broke some ribs at Talladega.

"Now here he was going to Daytona International Speedway to drive a hot Winston Cup car. I'll never forget it—he looked me in the eye and said, 'I can win that race.' I said, 'It will be a miracle if you even finish that race.' Oh, how I wish I had those words back."

Beth hurt for David. She smiled sympathetically, and she was pleased that he studied her blue eyes, her fair cheeks, her blonde Dutch boy bangs, and seemed calmed by what he saw.

But he took a deep breath and resumed the story. "So they went to Daytona, and Pete qualified that cheater car second, on the front row, barely missing winning the pole position. That jacked his confidence into the stratosphere. I groaned when I saw it on the TV news that night.

"I considered attending the race, since I live in Daytona Beach anyway. But I was afraid some reporter would spot me or fans would recognize me, and the questions would begin all over again, so I stayed home and watched on television.

"Pete took the lead in the first turn of the first lap, and then he began extending it. The fans were on their feet, waving him on as he came by the frontstretch grandstand. The TV announcers already were pronouncing him ready for a spot on Mount Olympus. I was muttering, 'Cool it, little brother, cool it.'

"He was a couple of hundred yards ahead of everyone when he crashed. He simply lost control and hit the outside concrete wall, practically head on. The race was in just its ninth lap.

"He was dead on arrival at the infield care center. NASCAR didn't announce it until after the race was over, but I knew he was dead as soon as I saw the wreck. It wasn't one of those spectacular flipping accidents. They disperse the energy and usually aren't so serious. It isn't how fast you go, it's how fast you stop, and Pete stopped fast when his car met that concrete wall. I telephoned a nurse friend who worked in the infield care center, and she confirmed that I had lost my brother.

"Herman Lanston had put him in a car he couldn't handle, in a situation he couldn't handle. One of the crewmen told me that Herman was on the radio himself, urging him to go faster, telling him he was going to be a better driver than his brother, and now was the time to show his stuff.

"The next day the papers quoted Lanston as saying he repeatedly told the unfortunate driver to slow down, to drive a tactical race, but that he wouldn't listen."

Chapter 10

Pappy Draper was holding court under the metal awning that extended from the rear of the massive tractor-trailer truck that served as a transporter of race cars, parts, and tools for the Bibley Designs racing team.

The vehicle also embraced a lounge of comfortable seats that was equipped with a TV set and a VCR, and David Marlow was in that oasis, away from the autograph seekers who trolled the garage areas of speedways, pouncing on any driver who showed his face.

It wasn't that Marlow was anti-autograph or unappreciative of the fans, for he'd signed his name thousands of times at the bullrings when his hands were red from the dust of the clay racing surface, and at the big league speedways. But so many fans were able to gain admittance to the garage areas as guests of sponsors that a driver simply had to escape every now and then. He was out of their reach in the garage itself or in the transporter, but the walk of thirty yards from the one to the other could mean a score of signings.

On this bright morning at North Carolina Speedway at Rockingham, David was content to leave center stage to his crew chief. The avid fans—as opposed to sponsors' clients making their first trip to a speedway—knew who Pappy was. The newspapers and racing tabloids wrote about him because he always had a colorful quote for them—and he never met a TV camera he didn't like.

A cluster of fans and press and other mechanics were engaged in repartee with Draper. "Yep, I used to soup up cars for the bootleggers and the revenuers when I was young and so many counties were dry," Draper said.

"Did you make one faster than the other?" a crewman asked. Beth recognized it as a set-up question, one he'd probably asked dozens of times before.

"Well, I'll put it this way," Pappy said. "If I did a five-hundred-dollar job for the bootlegger, he'd pay me in cash and tip me a couple hundred dollars. If I did a five-hundred-dollar job for the revenuer, I'd have to fill out forms in triplicate and send them to some government office, and maybe I'd get a check in ninety days and maybe I wouldn't.

"So which one would you have made faster?"

His audience howled and Pappy's face crinkled in unadulterated joy. He enjoyed making folks happy.

But showtime was over. Pappy motioned for Beth to follow him, and they disappeared into the transporter.

"Pretty funny stuff," she said.

"I've got two answers to that question I was asked," Pappy told her.

"What's the other one?"

"As long as the bootlegger could outrun the revenuer we all three had a job. So which one would you have made faster?"

"You're a mess," Beth said, and she wondered if the stories that linked the formative days of stock car racing with bootlegging were true.

"That's how the sport got started," Pappy said. "Whiskey trippers learned to drive the fire out of their cars—it was either that or get caught by the law—and it was only natural they'd scratch out race tracks in open fields all over the South and compete with each other to determine who had the fastest cars.

"Their races with the law on those winding mountain roads in

Georgia and North Carolina and Virginia were more dangerous than the organized races, though. They could pack a hundred and twenty gallons of moonshine in a 1940 Ford coupe that was powered by a big Cadillac motor, and handle it like it was a boy's car in a sandbox. A fellow who could make the bootleg turn could darn sure operate a race car."

"What's the bootleg turn?" Beth asked as Pappy painted four slices of bread with mayonnaise for their tomato sandwiches. The paper plates were smudged with auto grease, but that merely added to her sense of adventure. She spread a sheet of newspaper across a built-in workbench that would serve as their table, and then she took her seat on the top rung of a low stepladder that was used to retrieve parts and tools from cabinets and bins in the wall.

"Revenuers would be chasing a whiskey tripper, and up ahead other revenuers would put up a roadblock, usually by parking their cars nose to nose across the road," Pappy said.

"When he came up on the blockade the whiskey tripper would perform the bootleg turn. *At speed*, I mean. He'd put his right-side tires on the edge of the pavement, throw the gearshift up into second, jerk the handle of the emergency brake, and turn the steering wheel a quarter of a turn to the left, as quickly and as expertly as a card shark dealing off the bottom of the deck.

"The rear end would spin around, the tires screaming and producing a cloud of gray smoke. He'd bring the steering wheel back straight, let off the emergency brake, punch the accelerator, and he'd be headed back in the direction he came from. As he passed them, he'd probably wave at the laws who had been chasing him."

Pappy asked Beth if her tomato sandwich was okay and she said, "Delicious. I was starving." She wasn't surprised when he told her he grew the tomatoes himself.

"It was not only a game of speed but a battle of wits between the whiskey trippers and the authorities," Pappy continued.

"The lawmen would spot an unloaded car heading into the mountains to a still and they'd wait for it to come back, packed with 'shine. They'd step out of the bushes and shoot the radiator with a shotgun. Then they'd leisurely drive down the road a couple of miles to where the car had died from overheating. They'd tow it in and it would be auctioned in front of the courthouse on Saturday morning, and the sheriff or policeman who'd caught it would get half the money.

"So what do you reckon the whiskey trippers started doing? They put the radiator in the trunk and ran water hoses to the motor, and added air scoops to keep the contraption cool. They put a steel plate where the radiator used to be, and the shotgun pellets would just bounce off it. They'd drive on to Atlanta or wherever they were going to deliver their moonshine. It took the law quite awhile to figure out what was happening."

Hard-driving men and resourceful mechanics, Beth thought. Sounded mighty like stock car racing to her.

"The law came up with this thing they called a cowcatcher," Pappy said, "but it wasn't cows they planned to catch. It was mounted on the front of the police car, and it worked something like ice tongs.

"The law would bump the whiskey tripper from behind as he started up a steep hill, and the cowcatcher would grab the rear bumper. The law would ride the brakes, and both cars finally would come to a stop."

Beth knew he wanted her to ask how the bootleggers thwarted the cowcatcher, so she did.

"They started wiring their rear bumpers onto the car with coat hangers," Pappy said. "The cowcatcher would grab the bumper, but the bumper would pull off the car and the police car would get all tangled up in it. By the time they got untangled the whiskey tripper would be riding down Peachtree Street."

He certainly knew a lot about it, Beth thought. Should she ask? Of course, she should. "Pappy, you sound like a fellow who might have driven a moonshine run or two as a young man. Tell me, did you?"

He didn't hesitate. "Speaking of my tomatoes," Pappy said, "I used to win prizes with them at the county fair. I've still got a few blue ribbons in a scrapbook. I always had a magic touch with tomatoes—and corn, too, for that matter."

Beth laughed and Pappy continued his story of the evolution of stock car racing. Little coupes were specially modified for racing because they were light and fast, and dirt tracks proliferated. Then came paved short tracks. Late models that looked like the cars that transported Dad to work and the kids to school became the racing rage because of the identification factor, and *Win on Sunday, sell on Monday* was the catchphrase of the automobile manufacturers. Big, high-banked superspeedways were constructed, and the game had first-class facilities. Eventually every Winston Cup race would be televised and NASCAR would become a mainstream sport.

"It all goes back to Bill France Senior—Big Bill, as we called him," Pappy said. "He was the smartest man I ever met—and that includes four presidents of the United States."

He gazed out the back window, smiling faintly, obviously remembering some fond incident from the past that involved Big Bill France. Then he snapped his head to attention and said, "Like a lot of old folks, I talk about the past too much. I'm probably boring you."

"Nonsense," she said. "I want to hear about Big Bill. Tell me. And I'd like another tomato sandwich."

Pappy was delighted. "Well, Big Bill was the founder of NASCAR, the man who built the giant tracks at Daytona and Talladega. He was a giant himself, about six-foot-five. He had great charisma. He was a presence. When he walked into a room, the conversations stopped and everyone looked at him.

"Now, what's unusual is that he wasn't born into money. The only advantages he had were his fine mind and daring, and a willingness to work. What he didn't have that most of us have is tunnel vision. He saw how what happened today in Daytona Beach would impact what happened a few years later in California. He was a genius, but a genius with a marvelous, sincere personality.

"He didn't invent stock car racing, but he realized its potential and caused it to reach that potential. I'm convinced that if there had been no Big Bill France, stock car racing still would be nothing more than a bunch of amateurs dueling in battered hotrods on short tracks on Saturday night. I don't believe any other individual in the history of American sport was as important to his game as Big Bill was to stock car racing.

"When he died in 1992 at age eighty-two I sat down and cried, because if Big Bill hadn't made this sport I don't know where'd I'd be or what I'd be doing. I sure wouldn't be at a superspeedway preparing cars for a great driver and talking to a beautiful woman."

"You'd probably be *flirting* with a woman," Beth said, smiling. "It just wouldn't be me."

"Probably," Pappy agreed. "Anyway, Big Bill was born in Washington, D.C., and as a teenager he'd play hooky and go to the board track at Laurel, Maryland, and—"

Beth interrupted: "Board track?"

"Yes. Made out of wood. There were several of them in the U.S. This one was over a mile long. Big Bill even managed to slip the family car onto the track a few times. His dad used to complain to the tire dealer that the tires on the Model T sure did wear out in a hurry.

"Big Bill quit high school and went to work in a garage, even built a race car and started to drive some. He was working at a service station when he decided to move to Florida. One of his jobs was responding to calls from customers whose cars wouldn't start in the cold, and he decided that if he was going to have to repair cars for a living, he'd move to Florida where he wouldn't freeze to death.

"He and his family reached Daytona Beach, and he thought it was the prettiest place he'd ever seen, so that's where they stopped. Daytona had been a center of timed beach runs since 1902, so it was racing-oriented. Big Bill opened a filling station and it became a hangout for race drivers.

"They had had some races on a combination beach and highway course, but the races had flopped, and the chamber of commerce asked Big Bill if he knew someone who might promote the next race. He called a promoter he knew, but the guy refused the collect call, and that changed history. Big Bill decided to take a fling at it himself, and that's how his career as a promoter started. His beach-road races did well, and he began promoting at other tracks.

"Big Bill believed stock car racing would prosper if there was a framework to hold it together and give it uniform rules and purpose and guaranteed purses. There was a history of promoters skipping town with the prize money while the race was being run. So he organized the National Association for Stock Car Auto Racing.

"The first NASCAR race was run in 1948. It was for Modified cars, which were the typical stock cars of the day because they'd go fastest. They had souped-up motors and usually they were little coupes with some age on them.

"But France believed fans would turn out to see new sedans that looked like the ones they drove every day, so NASCAR added a series for them in 1949. Some folks said Big Bill was crazy—but that series is now called Winston Cup, and it defines stock car racing.

"France knew his new-car series would prosper if it had the right facilities, and he built Daytona International Speedway, which hosted the first Daytona 500 in 1959. That track truly lifted stock car racing to big-league status.

"Big Bill once got ushered out of the pits at mighty Indianapolis Motor Speedway. He said they resented the president of a rival association being in their pits. He never forgot it. He was trying to figure a way to get his Daytona track built, and that incident fired him up and made him go after it with a passion.

"He built Talladega Superspeedway in 1969. Another of his dreams that later materialized was the International Motorsports Hall of Fame at Talladega, which inducted its first class in 1990.

"NASCAR. Daytona. Talladega. The Hall of Fame. Not a bad lega-
cy for a former filling station mechanic. His son, Bill Junior, carried on
in the old man's footsteps, and the sport continued to grow."

Beth thanked Pappy for the tomato sandwiches and the history lesson. It was a long haul from bootleggers in whiskey-tripping cars on dirt
tracks to David Marlow in a modern racer on a superspeedway.

She wished David would step out of the tractor-trailer's lounge, and
she got her wish. He was yawning and wiping his eyes. "Beth! I didn't
know you were here. I needed that nap."

He embraced her and kissed her lightly on the forehead. "Dutch
Boy," he said.

"Dirt Dauber," she said.

She and David were okay again, and nothing could go wrong now. At
least that's what she thought.

Chapter 11

Vern Parchman had led the season's standings by a mere ten points entering the race at Talladega, but his victory, coupled with David Marlow's crash, left Parchman with a lead of 105 points over Marlow with four races to go. This in a system in which the champion was likely to accumulate some five thousand points.

Raider Slater, a third-year Winston Cup driver, had recorded six straight top-five finishes to leap into third place, just three points behind Marlow. David's pursuit was faltering, and he was becoming the pursued.

David had predicted in a newspaper interview that Slater would be a star if he ever learned to drive with his head instead of exclusively with his foot. He had been involved in several crashes because of impatience. "A driver doesn't have to win the race on the fifth lap," David had put it.

Shortly after that, he had seen Slater walking toward his garage stall at New Hampshire International Speedway, and he figured there would be harsh words, maybe a more serious incident. But Slater simply said he had read the story and that he appreciated the advice, and that he would indeed drive with more common sense.

The result of his reformation into a thinking driver had been the six consecutive top-five finishes—one of them a second place. Now he was nipping at David's heels in the points chase. "Me and my big mouth," David told Pappy. "Oh, well, no good deed goes unpunished."

It was as a bullring terror that Rudy Slater acquired his nickname. The Kentuckian read the racing trade papers, circled the stories about drivers who were dominating at their home tracks, then showed up unannounced at those speedways and, usually, outran the local hot-shots. He'd travel to Florida, Maine, North Carolina, California, and any point in between to prove his superiority.

It was a strategy designed to gain him national attention and a Winston Cup ride. It could be implemented because his father was a wealthy coal mining magnate and willing to pay the freight for top-flight race cars and all the trappings. Slater even had his own PR man, a savvy type who deluged the racing papers, the daily press, and television with stories of Slater's exploits.

"The guy raids your track, wins your money, and then vanishes into the night, never to be seen again," one anonymous (and fictitious) driver was quoted as saying. Anyway, the story provided Slater with an unforgettable nickname.

Slater had a fulltime ten-man crew—unheard of in bullring racing—that transported his cars over the nation while he flew in his dad's company jet. He was clever and colorful and in demand as an interview subject.

Sure enough, he caught the eye of a Winston Cup team owner and moneyed sponsor. His dad sweetened the pot by making his coal business an associate sponsor, and Slater was off and running on the big-time circuit.

Some drivers resented the silver spoon that was stuck squarely in Raider's perfect smiling teeth, but David wasn't one of them. Slater was smart enough to use his assets, and what was wrong with that? Besides, the handsome twenty-eight-year-old blond had uncommon talent, and now that he was harnessing it he was on his way to being a force in the big league.

Parchman, Marlow, and Slater were assembled at a media breakfast at the speedway in Rockingham to discuss the points chase. It was simpler than each one having to answer the same questions from a dozen reporters in the garage.

"Newspaper stories stir up interest in our sport, and I'm grateful for that," David told Beth privately before the proceedings commenced, "but I don't like being put in a position so that I have to lie."

"What do you mean?" she asked.

"If I catch Parchman in the points race, it probably will be because he either has mechanical failure or crashes, and gets a low position, just as I did at Talladega. Some reporter will ask if I want that to happen.

"Of course I want it to happen. It's part of racing, and it has a huge effect on the points standings. I hope his motor blows on the first lap. If it can't be mechanical failure, I hope he crashes. I'd say that even if he wasn't driving a cheater car. I don't want him to be injured, but I hope he goes out early. I'd be crazy not to.

"But I can't say that for publication. I'd be tarred as a poor sport who wants to back into the championship. Some of these holier-than-thou sports columnists aren't exactly eaten up with common sense."

Eggs, bacon, grits, and biscuits were consumed, and the press conference began. "We'll hear the drivers in reverse order," a PR man said. "First up will be the man who is third in points, Raider Slater."

"I'm just honored to be in the same room with these two great drivers," Slater said. "The Halcyon Home Products Pontiac team has provided me with outstanding cars. I'd also like to thank my associate sponsor, Cloudy Ridge Coal."

A veteran reporter sitting next to Beth groaned. "I could have stayed in the motel and watched commercials on TV," he whispered. "Typical racing crap." He obviously had anticipated the commercial, as he called it, for he had not removed his pad or pen from his pocket. Beth felt a little foolish for having jotted down Raider's words.

David and Parchman were introduced and they got in their plugs, too. It was humorous to watch them keep straight faces as they praised products like a couple of television infomercial pitchmen. "Okay," said the PR man, "the floor is open for questions. Please raise your hand and be recognized."

A young writer across the table from Beth raised his hand. The moderator pointed toward him and he said, "Raider, you're a young driver and you're unexpectedly in third place in the standings. Would you be satisfied with finishing third?"

What a stupid question, Beth thought.

Slater considered it for a full ten seconds, then said, "If I finish third, it will be higher than any of the experts predicted. But I dreamed of being the Winston Cup champion when I was a boy. Some kids wanted to be the winning pitcher in the seventh game of the World Series or throw the winning touchdown pass in the Super Bowl. I wanted to be the champion of NASCAR. I haven't fulfilled that dream yet."

The young reporter eagerly wrote down the glib reply, seemingly unaware that his question had not been answered.

Sure enough, the next question was the one David dreaded. "It will take some bad luck on Parchman's part for you to win the championship," a writer said. "Do you wish him bad luck?"

"No," David answered without hesitation. "The championship would mean more to me if I simply outran Vern on the track."

David couldn't help it. His eyes met Beth's and he laughed out loud. Everyone in the room turned to her, and she giggled like a schoolgirl.

She couldn't stop. All her life she had been subject to uncontrollable laughter. Once she had been sent to the principal's office because she had had a laughing fit when she spotted the unzipped fly of a teacher who stood before the class at a blackboard.

The more she laughed, the more David laughed. The absurdity of their answers struck Raider Slater, and he began laughing, too.

Vern Parchman glanced from Raider to David to Beth. "Am I missing something?" he said dourly.

"It was just a little inside joke, nothing to do with racing at all," David lied, straightening his face. Beth pinched her arm until it hurt and made herself stop laughing. She silently thanked David for bailing her out.

The flustered moderator pronounced, "We're adjourned. If you want to talk to the drivers one-on-one, I'm sure they'll stick around for a few minutes."

Beth had an idea for a story. She would turn the vapid quotes to her advantage. She'd write about the insipid replies to the reporters' questions and explain why they're standard fare at racing press conferences. Charlie Murphy had never done that.

She asked the drivers more pointed questions and listened as other reporters did the same. She marveled at their ability to answer without really answering.

"The speedway will be open for practice in ten minutes," the PR man said. "The drivers have to go. Thanks to all for attending today's press conference."

Beth liked Raider Slater. She knew he had been considered a lively, controversial interview subject when he was a vagabond short track terror, but now he seemed as programmed as a politician running for office. "I know you have to practice, but I wonder if I might chat with you afterward?" she asked Slater.

"Sure," he said. "You're Beth Barrett of *The Birmingham News*, right?"

"Why, yes." She smiled quizzically.

"You're wondering how I knew," he said. "Well, let me put it this way. If you had been *Bill* Barrett of *The Birmingham News*, I wouldn't have known."

He was funny. She wished she could pull for him to win the championship. Oh, well, she could pull for him to finish second to David and ahead of Vern Parchman. Or, more precisely, ahead of Herman Lanston's interests.

Slater said he'd meet her at his garage stall after practice and they'd talk. Beth thanked him and strolled along the line of race cars, but they hadn't been separated for two minutes when she heard Slater's voice. "Beth, my car isn't ready for practice. The crew chief has decided to change motors. We can chat now if you like."

"Great," she said.

"Let's stand over here between these transporters," Slater said. "I'm tired of sitting, and I'd like to breathe some fresh air."

"Me, too," she said, and they welcomed the sunshine that wedged between the huge trucks and moderated the October chill.

She explained what she wanted. She told Slater she had covered ball sports, where the press conferences could get pretty lively. But she had noticed racing press conferences seemed to just "lie there." Could he tell her why?

Slater considered her request for a moment, then said, "I'll talk to you if you don't identify me. You can quote a driver who asked that his name not be used, or however y'all do it. Is that agreeable?"

"Well, uh, I guess so," she said.

"Okay. On a given Sunday, forty-three drivers will start a Winston Cup race. But thirteen hundred men play NFL football and seven hundred will play major league baseball. This is an elite sport. It's difficult to make stock car racing's big league, and difficult to stay there.

"Professional ballplayers don't have to answer to anybody. They can be as trashy as they choose to be, say anything they want to say. They can be thugs. They don't have sponsors."

The race cars pulled onto the speedway and their roar overwhelmed Slater's words. Beth leaned in to hear him, and he revved up his voice to meet the revving of motors.

"It costs a fortune to run a Winston Cup team for a season." Slater continued. "Say a sponsor is supplying fifteen million dollars to keep the wheels spinning and the motor running—well, that sponsor has a lot of influence with the team owner. No sponsor, no team.

"Now, don't name my sponsor in your story, because that would identify me, but Halcyon Home Products makes cleansers, soap, starch, bleach, all sorts of products a homemaker has in her kitchen and laundry room.

"Halcyon would not appreciate my big mouth creating a controversy that might reflect poorly on its goods and send Mamma to a competitor's stuff in the supermarket. My team owner would not appreciate my making Halcyon anything but a happy camper.

"I'm one of those elite forty-three, and I'm not going to blow that, so I lean too far in the other direction. And believe me, what you saw and heard in there today isn't the real me. I'd love to speak my mind—after all, that's how I got to Winston Cup, by being a colorful, outspoken character—but I can't."

Beth flipped the page in her notebook, wrote the word *Pappy*, and circled it. "Pappy Draper is a colorful, outspoken character," she said. "He isn't so cautious."

"Pappy is the exception who proves the rule," Slater said. "He's a link to racing's wild old days. Bibley Design's customers expect him to be a grizzled oddity out of the pages of folklore.

"Pappy talks about helping the whiskey trippers of a half-century ago. They're romantic figures like the pirates you read about when you were a kid. But if he said he helped modern-day drug runners, he'd be a pariah. If David Marlow said he engaged in some illegal activity between races, he'd be out on his ear in a second."

Beth nodded. "Makes sense," she said.

"Stock car fans have incredible product loyalty," Slater continued. "That's why so many companies . . ."

The scream of tires being wrenched sideways under sliding cars, and the bang of cars colliding with each other and the concrete wall, caused Beth to jump and drop her notebook.

"There's a three-car crash in the fourth turn!" the public address announcer shouted. "Wait! One has burst into flames! It's a white car. I believe it's David Marlow's."

"Oh, God, no!" Beth screamed. Standing in the canyon created by the two huge transporters, she couldn't see the track. She ran in front of the trucks, but the buildings blocked her view. She saw a metal ladder on the side of a transporter and began climbing it. "Careful!" Raider Slater yelled. "These ladders are tricky. I'm right behind you."

Now she stood atop the truck and she peered around a man in sunglasses and wide-brimmed straw hat and mechanic's overalls, who had been clocking the racers with a stopwatch. A white car was engulfed in flames. She screamed and grabbed the rail that spanned the width of the truck, lending support to her legs that trembled like dandelion stems in the wind.

"I stand corrected!" the public address announcer said. "The burning car is not David Marlow's. It's Wilford Raleigh's, and Raleigh is out of the car and waving his hand, signaling he is okay. Sharman Garard and Vern Parchman are the other two drivers, and they aren't injured either."

"Thank God," the man in the sunglasses and straw hat and overalls said, and he opened his arms to Beth, who fell into them.

"Yes, yes, thank God," she said, laughing and crying at the same time. She hugged the man and buried her face on his shoulder. She wiped the tears from her eyes with the sleeve of her sweater, and only then did she realize the man she was embracing and who was embracing her was Herman Lanston.

Chapter 12

*T*he voice on the telephone said, "Guess who?"

It was weak, rasping, but Beth recognized the twang and the optimistic, unconquerable lilt that accompanied it, and decided she should answer in kind. "I know who," she said. "Arnie, how in the world are you? You sound great."

"I am great," Arnie Shale groaned. "That is, if you don't count a busted arm, a busted leg, a busted cheekbone, a busted breastbone, some busted ribs, and a brain that's running on seven cylinders, maybe six. I keep calling the IV in my arm a VCR and Birmingham Bethlehem, but the doc says I'll mend and my brain will work perfect. I told him that's wonderful, because it never worked perfect before the crash. Maybe if I wreck again I'll be an Einstein."

Beth laughed, but the catch in her voice betrayed her, and Arnie said, "Aw, don't cry. I ain't really going to ever be no Einstein."

She laughed and cried and said, "I'm just so thrilled to hear your voice. I didn't know whether you'd ever . . ."

"I understand," he said. "That's why I called you. You're a caring person, and I wanted to talk to you. Herman Lanston gave you that scoop that Vern Parchman is retiring, and I wanted to give you the scoop that Arnie Shale ain't taking that early retirement to the Pearly Gates quite yet."

"Your paper kept sending this young reporter over to the hospital every day to check on me. I finally regained consciousness today, and I heard him agreeing with my mother that racing is crazy, so I knew I wasn't about to talk to him.

"I called your sports editor and asked him which motel you were at in Rockingham, and I guess I sounded like some pervert, gasping and moaning and all, and he didn't want to tell me. I let him know who I was, and he said he'd send a reporter right over to talk to me, but I said no, I wanted you. So he gave me the motel."

His voice was weakening, and Beth heard another voice in the background say, "All right, Mr. Shale, that's enough for tonight." Arnie protested and the voice said, "Well, keep it short."

"That's the doctor," he told Beth. "I am getting tired, and I've got the grandpaw of headaches. Anyway, tell the public I'm getting better and the *St. Clair County Special* will be back on the track next season."

"Take care, Arnie," she said. "I'm so happy you're, uh, improving." She meant she was happy he was alive, because every time the phone rang she had feared it was Blake Watkins informing her he was dead.

Beth asked to speak to the doctor, who told her he was pleasantly surprised by Arnie's progress, but that he was still a very sick young man and he would be hospitalized indefinitely.

"Then he's certain to live?" Beth asked, repulsed by the bluntness of the necessary question.

"As certain as any of us," the doctor said impatiently. "I've got to make my rounds now."

Beth phoned Blake Watkins, told him she would have a story saying Arnie had regained consciousness, and began typing on her laptop. She hadn't finished the first paragraph when there was a knock on her door.

"Hi, Dutch Boy," David Marlow said. The sight of the dark, handsome man in jeans and an ochre golf shirt, framed in the doorway of her room, filled her with joy.

"David, I have the most wonderful news," she said. "Arnie Shale regained consciousness today. He just phoned me."

She couldn't help it. She was so happy, so overcome by the good news and the presence of the man she loved that she pressed her face against his chest to hide the tears of joy.

David held her close. His hand rubbed the back of her head, patted the short-cropped hair, then he kissed her eyelids, as gently as an autumn breeze.

Beth wiped her eyes with the back of her hand and said, "Now look at your pretty shirt. I drowned it, Dirt Dauber."

He kissed her lips, pressed her to him. "I never knew drowning could be so nice," he said.

David nodded toward the laptop screen, alight with the first words of her story. "Better not miss another deadline," he said. "Your sports editor might assign you to cover golf, and I wouldn't like that."

"Neither would I," Beth said. "For some reason I've become quite attached to covering stock car racing."

David watched the news on TV while Beth finished her story on Arnie Shale. The sports anchor told the viewing audience that Raider Slater had won the pole position for the next day's four-hundred-mile Winston Cup race at North Carolina Speedway. David qualified second, Vern Parchman third.

"Raider's team scares me," David said. "They've really come together lately. He's driving a saner race, and that has inspired his crewmen. It can be pretty disheartening when your driver is always tearing the car up in some dumbo wreck. That's off the record, of course."

"Of course," Beth said, "but now I need something on the record for my story—a quote from you on Arnie's recovery."

"I was delighted to hear he had regained consciousness," David said in the effortless delivery of a celebrity accustomed to being quoted. "Arnie Shale is a courageous, determined young race driver. I'm confident he will return to Winston Cup racing."

Beth typed in David's words and said, "Now I know why I like covering racing. The star comes by your motel room in case you need aquote for a story."

"I'll bet quarterbacks and shortstops don't do that," David said.

Beth enjoyed the easy repartee with David and it was obvious he did, too. The Winston Cup star was still the same sweet guy who had churned up the clay of the Alabama dirt tracks.

She attached the telephone line to her computer and transmitted her story to the newspaper's computer system. Then she and David left for dinner at a hole-in-the-wall barbecue joint.

Just as the owner of the Italian restaurant had done, the owner of the barbecue place sat them in a back room, away from the other customers, who would surely bother David for autographs, always prefacing their greeting with, "I hate to bother you while you're eating, but . . ." They didn't hate it so much that they didn't do it.

"This pork is delicious," Beth said.

"There's nothing better than good barbecue and nothing worse than bad barbecue," David said. "This is the real stuff, smoked for hours, all the fat trimmed off, the sauce perfect. I love barbecue and I know all the best Q joints on the circuit. Sometimes they aren't much to look at, but the food is more important than the looking."

Beth liked that. She always considered the food more important than the looking, too. And it was further evidence that celebrity hadn't gone to David's head.

"What do you see for tomorrow?" Beth asked him. "Off the record, of course."

"I see a wide open, unpredictable race," he answered. "A lot of guys are really dialed in for this one. The practice and qualifying speeds show that. Unfortunately, you could run a fine race and still finish fifteenth.

"If Parchman won and I finished fifteenth, he'd pick up, oh, sixty-two points on me, and I'd be all but cooked in the points chase. Of course, if I won and he finished fifteenth I'd be back in the hunt. As you know, he leads me by one hundred and five points with four races to go, including this one. Slater is just three points behind me. Of course, what I hope is that they both drop out early."

David gasped and covered his mouth with his hand. "Shame on me," he kidded. "I meant to say I don't wish them any bad luck, and I hope they stay in the race until the end because the championship would mean more to me that way."

Beth patted his hand. She noted his fingernails were clipped and clean. He was in a dirty, greasy profession, but off the track David was clean and well groomed. He had been when he was racing on dirt tracks, and he was now.

"I hope you get your championship," she said. "I know how much it means to you."

David took her hand in his and said, "Actually, you don't. I didn't tell you everything about Herman Lanston. There was a postscript after my brother Pete was killed driving his car at Daytona."

"A postscript?"

"Beth, Lanston is garbage, the lowest form of human life. I want to deny him the championship as much as I want to win it.

"As I told you, my brother was twenty years old when he was killed driving Lanston's car. He left a nineteen-year-old widow, Joy. Like any couple that age, they didn't have anything. And now Joy was left without a husband but with a seven-month-old daughter.

"Joy was—is—a beautiful girl, and that wasn't lost on Lanston. He told her he wanted to help financially, since Pete was killed driving his car. He visited a couple of times and spoke of giving her a job with Lanston Farms, even setting up a trust fund for the baby.

"Then he hit on her and she gave in to him. I assume she felt she had to protect her child's future, and that would do it.

"Anyway, he quickly tired of her. He laughed and told some of his crewmen she was too gloomy for him. He said he learned a lesson—that a fellow should never go to bed with a brand new widow who still loved her husband. The story made the rounds in racing. She didn't get a job, and the baby didn't get a trust fund.

"Joy was crushed. She did love Pete, but she realized everyone in racing knew she had gone to bed with Herman Lanston.

"I had offered to help her—support her, really—before Lanston made his move, but Pete's animosity toward me had transferred to her. All she knew about our differences was Pete's version. She believed, because he did, that I was trying to keep him down. Maybe that was another reason she felt she had no choice but to go to bed with Lanston.

"After Lanston bailed out, I assured her my offer was still open, but she wouldn't accept it. Now she's a waitress in some hash house, living from hand to mouth."

Herman Lanston had been so courtly and attentive to Beth. Well, it was obvious where he intended their relationship to lead. "Calling him garbage is slandering garbage," she told David.

"Well, we'd better call it a night," David said. "I need a good night's sleep to go four hundred miles at Rockingham."

He drove her to her motel, kissed her long and tenderly in the doorway of her room, and said, "Write a good story about me winning tomorrow, Dutch Boy."

"I'll do that," she told him as he skipped down the stairs from the second floor—and, smiling at the thought of how unsuitable the nickname was for a handsome star of big league racing, she added, "my Dirt Dauber."

OCTOBER IN NORTH Carolina was special. "Golden October had come again," one of its favorite sons, author Thomas Wolfe, wrote. The sentence had stuck in Beth's mind from the first time she read it, when she was in high school. It was simple, but its promise of the cycle of nature was somehow reassuring.

Race day couldn't have been more gorgeous. The sky was cloudless blue—Tar Heel blue, fans of the University of North Carolina called it. "If God isn't a Tar Heel, why did he make the sky Tar Heel blue?" they reasoned. The leaves were beginning to assume their yellow and red and orange hues.

Beth arrived at the track, stowed her laptop at her spot in the press box, and went to the garage area.

Crewmen were on, in, and under cars, making final preparations for the carnival-colored machines to travel four hundred miles quickly and reliably. She wondered how there could be that much to do at this late hour.

Vern Parchman passed her, walking fast, looking straight ahead. He glanced at her but there was no sign of recognition. He didn't recognize the woman who had written the scoop about his retirement.

She hated it when anyone said "the media" does this or that, or thinks this or that. Members of the media are as varied as any other group. But she realized that to many, probably including Vern Parchman, they were just one big lump.

"I hate the media," a football coach had once told her. She asked if that meant he hated Oprah Winfrey, the local weatherman, the editor of a Baptist newspaper, and her sports editor. He'd simply turned and walked away.

Pappy Draper didn't hate "the media." He was entertaining a wide-eyed young reporter who was furiously making notes. He winked as Beth joined them.

"I caught a possum in a trap and put it in the backseat of the 1950 Buick I towed the race car with, and headed off to Daytona for Speed Weeks," he said. "About halfway there I stopped at this little old mom and pop motel, and that night, when nobody was looking, I tied the possum under the bed.

"I phoned the manager and told him there was a mouse in my room and would he please come and catch it because I was afraid of mice.

"He came to the room, and I said it was under the bed, and he said he couldn't believe a grown man was afraid of a mouse.

"He got down on his belly and slithered up under that bed. He saw that possum, and he screamed and busted his head on a slat and hightailed it out of that room. Caught the pink chenille bedspread on his jacket button and drug it all the way across the parking lot.

"In a few minutes he came back all furious-like and said he was going to *whup* me, but I gave him a drink of my Jack Daniel's, and he settled down and even offered to buy the possum so he could play the same joke on his wife. I gave it to him free of charge, and he knocked fifty cents off the motel bill."

The young reporter was having the time of his life, no doubt picturing his editor praising him for the anecdotal article he would write about Pappy Draper. "Got any more stories?" he asked.

"Not over a million," Pappy said. "I'll tell you how I won twenty-five bucks one time—and this was back when twenty-five bucks was a lot of money.

"I was working on a 1939 Ford coupe, and I had the engine out. I bet a buddy I could get the car to a town seventeen miles away, that's without an engine or towing it.

"I pushed it out to the side of the highway and flagged down a fellow in a pickup truck. I told him my car wouldn't start, and would he give me a push? He pushed and pushed and pushed, and then he rolled up beside me and said he didn't believe it was going to start. I told him it almost started there one time, and if he'd push again I thought it would start. He pushed some more, and he got frustrated and said it wasn't going to start. I talked him into pushing again. Finally he just threw up his hands and touched the brake and let me roll on and drove away, not even looking my way.

"I flagged down an old boy in the worst-looking car you ever saw and got him to push me. Same thing happened. Then I flagged down another one and another one and about ten more, and after about five hours I had traveled that seventeen miles and made myself twenty-five bucks."

Pappy waited for the young reporter to ask the obvious question, but he didn't. "Heck of it was, I was seventeen miles from home in a car with no engine. I had to pay a wrecker driver twenty-five bucks to haul me and the car back home."

"Pappy, where's David?" Beth asked.

"He's flitting around somewhere. He'll have to come by eventually."

She listened to Pappy's stories for a few minutes, and then she saw David approaching. He was smiling—but the smile was too broad, artificial. "Why, Beth Barrett!" he said. "How in the world are you getting along, girl!"

It was a strange greeting. "Good morning, David," she said tentatively.

"I guess I should call you Mata Hari instead of Beth Barrett," he said, the lilt still in his voice. "I do want you to know that I'm past the point of even being angry. Sometimes when a person is totally defeated, he becomes resigned, not angry.

"But I do wish you would tell me how the girl I knew back in Alabama was reincarnated as a spy for Herman Lanston. How is it possible for you to say the things you said to me, and to listen to me say the things I said to you, and for you to carry it off so convincingly? As they say, you ought to be in *pictures*, girl."

"David, I don't know what . . ."

David unrolled an eight-by-ten photograph and said, "I'm going to have this framed as a reminder that I shouldn't be so naive. But, as I said, I'm not angry; I'm just amazed."

The photograph showed Herman Lanston holding Beth against him. Both were smiling.

She was stunned. Then she remembered. When she thought David's car had crashed and that it was on fire, she had scurried up the ladder to the top of Lanston's race car transporter. When she had learned David wasn't injured, she had hugged the man in mechanic's overalls, straw hat, and sunglasses, without realizing it was Lanston.

"And please don't insult my intelligence by telling me this picture was made at Talladega before you learned what a scumbag Lanston is," David said, forcing his theatrical smile even wider. "It was made at this track, because I recognize the grandstand in the background, and it was made yesterday, because those are the clothes you had on yesterday and those are the clothes Lanston had on yesterday."

She grasped his arm and began, "David, let me explain how this . . ."

But he shook off her hand, turned his back on her and began talking to one of his crewmen, both their heads under the hood of the car.

Beth felt as if her head were on the block of a guillotine.

Chapter 13

*T*he gentlemen started their engines, but as the pace laps began, Beth didn't look up from her workplace in the press box. She gazed at another print of the offending photograph. This one had been displayed on the bulletin board in the press box before she removed it.

Who would have snapped the photo? And why? It portrayed the most incriminating split second of her brief encounter with Herman Lanston. That meant the photographer probably shot rapid fire and then picked the most damning of the pictures.

Was it one of Lanston's men? The car owner's mean streak certainly would extend to breaking up the romance that was budding between David and herself. But Lanston couldn't have known she would climb that ladder at that moment, and that the opportunity for such a photo would present itself.

Was it a photographer for another newspaper? But why would a colleague care one way or the other what she did? She wasn't Princess Diana, hounded by the paparazzi.

The green flag waved and forty-three cars accelerated on the frontstretch of North Carolina Speedway. Beth tucked the photo into her briefcase.

Turn left on green. David liked to say that was what he did for a living, and as he turned left for the first time in this race he was in the lead. He extended his advantage over Raider Slater to fifty yards on the backstretch. Beth wondered if he thought of the gas pedal as her face as he jammed it to the floorboard.

A driver could earn five bonus points by leading a lap and five more by leading the most laps. David picked up the first bonus by leading the opening lap. She wondered if he planned to drive flat-out the entire race in a quest for the second bonus. It would be risky, but perhaps he was so far behind Vern Parchman—105 points in the standings—that he felt it was necessary.

David had told her he didn't like the points system. He felt it should put more of a premium on winning races, that there should be a larger difference in the number of points earned by the winner and the run-nerup.

The winner got 175 points, and there was a drop of five points per position through sixth place, then a drop of four per position through eleventh place, then a drop of three through the rest of the positions. Figure in the bonus points, and it was actually possible for the second-place finisher in a race to come away with as many points as the winner got.

The points system rewarded consistency more than victory. A driver could win five races, lead the most laps in each one, and then finish thirty-fifth in a race because he made a daring move in an attempt at another victory, and find himself behind in the points to a driver who fished third in each of the six races and never led a lap.

Beth tried to get her mind off the photo and onto the points standings by jotting down several possibilities—if Parchman finished in this position and David finished in this position and Slater finished in this position, etc. But it was impossible. There was something about a fractured heart that didn't lend itself to doing arithmetic.

"What's Marlow trying to do," the writer next to her said, "lap the field in the first ten minutes? He may not be around for the finish, and he can't stand another DNF."

If David did punish his car to the breaking point she would feel it was because he was exasperated with her. If that happened, she might never have an opportunity to explain. Of course, she might never have an opportunity to explain anyway.

After seven laps David was nearly a straightaway ahead of the field. Slater was running second. Parchman, driving a characteristic race, was lagging in twelfth place.

A rookie driver tried to pass on the inside in the third turn, but he had too much momentum and his car veered up against the one beside it. The first one spun into the inside retaining wall, the second tagged the outside wall. Two more cars crashed while trying to avoid the melee. The yellow caution flag waved. Four cars were out of the race before the engines were hot enough to melt ice cream, as Pappy Draper would say, and David's lead evaporated.

The cars crept around North Carolina Speedway while wreckers removed the cars that had crashed and cleanup crews swept the debris from the track. Spectators stretched and headed for the restrooms.

Beth tuned her scanner to intercept the conversation between David and Pappy. That was one advantage a racing writer or even a racing fan had over those in other sports: he or she could eavesdrop while a "player" and a "coach" chatted during the action.

"The car's perfect," David told Pappy. "It's handling like a dream, and the motor's pouring out the horsepower. I can drive any line on the track, at least so far."

"You were pretty aggressive," Pappy said. "Don't overdo it."

"This car is like a spirited thoroughbred," David explained. "It runs better if you turn it loose. This Ford is an athlete, Pappy. You've out-done yourself this time."

The green flag waved, David turned left, and again the car zipped away from the field. His fans were standing and cheering and waving him on as he passed the frontstretch stands and completed the lap.

"Tire's going down. I must have run over some debris from the wreck. Can you believe this? It's going to make for a long day, Pappy. I'm coming in. I think it's the right rear, but let's change all four to be sure."

David slowed and dropped to the apron. It was a long way back to the pits, and the erstwhile leader seemed to be moving at a glacial pace as the field roared by, with Raider Slater on the point.

Beth tuned her scanner to Vern Parchman's frequency. She clenched her jaw as Herman Lanston said, "Ain't that a shame? Marlow was running so well, too. Gee, I hate that." His laugh was humorless, more a grunt than a laugh. "How is it with you, my boy?" Lanston asked Parchman.

"No problems," the driver said. "I'm right where I want to be. Let Slater and the others run themselves into the ground. I'm going high through the third turn in case there's more garbage on the track."

David's car reached the entrance to pit road and coasted to a stop between the painted lines that marked his station. His crew sprang into action, men, tires, air wrenches, and fuel cans in a ballet that proceeded so quickly it defied delineation by spectators. He was out of his pit in a tick more than fifteen seconds.

Still, by the time his car left pit road and got back up to speed, David was more than two laps behind. "No way to make that up, even with practically all the race still to be run," the reporter sitting next to Beth said.

"You won't have to worry about Marlow," Beth heard Lanston tell Parchman. "He'll ride it out and pick up what points he can."

Parchman's snicker was audible. "Boss, that's wishful thinking," he said. "You're nuts if you think Marlow's going to give up now."

Beth was shocked by the words and the tone of Parchman's voice. A writer sitting on the row in front of her held a scanner, too, and she saw him grin, so she wasn't alone in her surprise.

"Don't you ever say I'm nuts!" Lanston told the driver. "You'd do well to remember who's the employer and who's the employee."

"Sorry," Parchman said. "Just a figure of speech."

Was there a crack in the relationship of Herman Lanston and Vern Parchman, she wondered? Probably not, but it was an interesting exchange.

David moved up through the field, picking off car after car. His advance was spectacular in the results it was achieving but methodical in execution. He wasn't reckless, wasn't taking chances. If a driver crowded him, he backed off. He picked his spots. Vern Parchman gave him ample room, and he dropped the Bibley Designs Ford in front of the Lanston Farms Chevrolet.

"You should have made him earn that!" Beth heard Herman Lanston tell his driver.

"I'm leading the standings by a hundred and five points and I should be contesting a guy who's two laps behind?" Parchman shot back. "Come on, Herman!"

Lanston didn't answer. Perhaps he realized how foolish his advice was. But Beth reckoned his anger toward Parchman shot up a few degrees.

The exchange between Lanston and Parchman underscored the animosity between Lanston and David Marlow. Beth was perplexed, but she understood David's reaction to the mysterious photograph. Had the man in the picture been anyone but Lanston, David might have been puzzled, miffed, but he would have given her a chance to explain. But there were no gray areas where Lanston was concerned. David could only see her as Lanston's mistress, sent to spy on the driver Lanston hated, shamelessly using their relationship of years past to gain David's trust. David was deeply wounded.

David picked off four cars in one lap and his fans were on their feet, waving caps, flags, towels, shirts. Two laps later he was on the bumper of Raider Slater, the leader.

"Remember his past history," Pappy Draper told his driver over the radio. "I know he's been driving more sensibly lately, but he might revert to his old ways in this situation. He can be a wild young buck."

"Good point," David said. "I'll be careful."

David drove into the bottom lane. So did Slater. David pulled up a lane. So did Slater. The youngster didn't care if the veteran was two laps behind; he wasn't going to give him a free pass.

David rode behind Slater for three laps before a desirable situation presented itself. A car that had been lapped several times was riding in a middle lane. As they approached it, David feinted to the inside. Slater bit and moved low, and when the right front quarter panel of Slater's car was beside the left rear quarter panel of the lapped car, David cranked his steering wheel to the right and passed both the lapped car and Slater's Chevy.

Even someone as new to racing as Beth was could appreciate what she'd just seen.

"Great move!" Pappy Draper told his driver.

"I averaged twenty points a game playing high school basketball," David said. "You don't do that without learning to use your picks."

Beth tuned in Slater's frequency in time to hear the young driver tell his crew chief, "Aw, what the heck, he's still way behind."

She recognized a whistling-past-the-graveyard quality in his voice, though. Slater had to be thinking that if David could regain one lap, he could perhaps regain two and eventually pass him a third time for the lead. A long afternoon lay ahead of them.

Beth hoped for a caution period that would allow David to make up lost ground, but the green stayed out. Their pit stop times were even, so David couldn't gain on Slater in that regard, but David was advancing on the track, and again he was on Vern Parchman's rear bumper.

"Put him in the wall!" Herman Lanston screamed into his radio as David's car drew even with Parchman's.

"You're crazy, Herman," Parchman said as David made a clean pass. "Man, don't you know this ain't exactly a private conversation we're having?"

Beth watched through her binoculars as a NASCAR official

approached Parchman's pit. The official was wagging his finger and yelling at Lanston. Indeed, it hadn't been a private conversation.

Lanston smiled and shook his head and held up both hands, a gesture no doubt calculated to assure the official he simply got carried away. The official chewed him out and then, on his own radio, assured the control tower he had issued the reprimand.

Lanston's smile vanished and in a measured tone he told his driver, "I'll deal with you later."

Slater had swapped the lead with a couple of other drivers, but he was back in front when David again reached his rear bumper. The spectators were screaming, waving Marlow on. Seeing a driver make up two laps under green was as rare as seeing a baseball player hit three home runs in one game

Again Slater threw a block, but this time Marlow slammed his rear bumper. It wasn't enough to upset Slater's line, but it announced that the name of the second chapter in this game would not be cat and mouse, as the first had been. Marlow didn't intend to wait for a lapped car to set a pick. Instead, the cleanup crew might scrape Slater's car off the wall if he didn't give his pursuer room.

Slater moved over and allowed David to unlap himself. The paying customers stood on their seats, shaking their fists at the sky, their chorus of cheers trumping the roar of the engines.

"Mr. Marlow just reminded Mr. Slater that Mr. Slater has a chance to win the first Winston Cup race of his career, and Mr. Slater would be stupid to jeopardize it by trying to bully Mr. Marlow, who is far in arrears," the reporter beside Beth said. She was pleased that her growing powers of racing deduction had led her to that exact conclusion.

David was back in the lead lap, but he was at its tail end. He was riding mere yards in front of Slater, but in reality he was still nearly a mile behind him.

Caution flags are as much a part of Winston Cup racing as American flags are a part of the Fourth of July, but this race had been unusual in that it had proceeded for so long under green. It reached the final twenty-four laps before the second yellow waved. It was the first caution period since the rookie had caused the crash on the sixth lap.

That was the break David needed. He had a free pass to catch up to the leaders. Everyone pitted and came out with four new tires, ready for the showdown.

When the green flag waved, Slater was in front, Parchman was second and David was twelfth, the last driver on the lead lap.

Beth clenched her pen so tightly that it broke and ink ran down her hand onto her wrist. She feared that the terrific pace David had been forced to maintain all day had weakened his car, that it might not have the power needed to complete his magnificent comeback.

David passed four cars on the first green lap. He passed six more on the next three laps, and now he was third, behind Vern Parchman, who was behind Raider Slater.

"You're second in class," Pappy told David on the radio. "Now show Parchman you can overcome his advantage."

Beth understood what the cryptic message, with its reference to sports car "class" racing, meant. David's "class" was that of legal cars. Slater's was legal and so was David's, but Parchman had the built-in advantages of Lanston's cheater car.

"I'm going to spectate for a few laps," David said. "I've got a hunch I'm in the best seat in the house for a really big show."

Beth wondered what he was saying. She thought David would need all the remaining laps to pass both Parchman and Slater.

Parchman was driving inches off Slater's bumper, putting tremendous pressure on the young driver, playing a mind game. Every fan was standing, yelling and waving on his or her particular favorite.

Parchman tried to drive inside Slater but Slater closed the door. He tried to drive outside Slater, but Slater closed the door. Inside, outside, inside, outside—nothing worked.

The words of Herman Lanston to his driver were delivered in the manner of a schoolmaster calmly but firmly instructing a student: "You had better win this race. Second place is the first loser."

Parchman drove to the outside of Slater—this time so far up the bank of the third turn that Slater didn't bother to block him. If he was running no more than a certain speed, the extra distance would prevent his passing Slater. If he was running more than that speed, he would crash.

He crashed.

Parchman lost control and his car hit the outside concrete wall. It veered off the wall into another car, and the caution flag waved.

To pit or not to pit? Did a driver take on four new tires under caution or did he protect his position on the track? Crew chiefs figured the green would wave with eight laps to go. What to do?

Obviously, the cars at the end of the lead lap would opt for new tires. They had nothing to lose, everything to gain. But if Slater pitted for new rubber he surely would lose the lead and might never regain it. David might win the race on new tires—or if he pitted he might never get as high as second place again. If he didn't take on new tires, one or more of the cars in arrears that did might pass him.

"Slater won't pit," David told Pappy. "I could use new tires, but I'm staying out, too."

"You don't have to win the race," Pappy said. "Parchman's assured of a bad finish and you can gain a lot of points by finishing second or third. Why don't you get the tires?"

Beth heard David's chuckle. He said, "You know me better than that, Pappy."

The green flag waved and Slater drove hard into the first turn. David didn't challenge him. When the cars returned to the start-finish line, Slater was a hundred yards ahead of the field.

He increased his lead by another fifty yards on the backstretch, but then his car wiggled in the third turn. Two laps later, David passed him for the lead. Then two more cars shot by Slater, and he was in fourth place.

"Raider did just what I thought he would do," David told Pappy. "He got overeager and killed his tires. I let mine cool off. I hope I've got enough rubber for the finish."

He did have. He held off a young driver from Iowa by blatantly blocking the track. An older, more experienced man might have mixed it with David but he figured—correctly—that this lad wouldn't, and he didn't.

The winning driver and his crew chief came to the press box for the postrace interview. David never made eye contact with Beth. Neither did Draper, and that told her Pappy had seen the photograph and had believed his eyes.

"This was the best race car I've ever driven," David told the press. "Pappy Draper is a genius. I owe him an apology, because earlier in the week I called this car a piece of junk. It was more than up to the challenge today."

It had been an eventful, memorable race, and the press had plenty of questions. David and Pappy answered them all. Beth thought it better if she kept quiet, so she asked nothing. There were plenty of quotes without her questions.

"Were you pleased to see Vern Parchman crash near the end?" came the inevitable question. "You gained a lot of ground in the points standings."

David smiled faintly and considered all the implications. Then he answered, "I thought it was great."

Chapter 14

Beth winced when she saw Arnie Shale in the hospital bed. His broken arm was in a cast, and so was his broken leg. His face was bruised purple and one eye was bloodshot. A laceration across his chin had been stitched.

"All this scene needs is a caption," Arnie said. "You've seen the cartoons with the patient all broke up and a funny line written underneath? You're a writer. Write something funny for this picture."

At least the young driver had clung to his sense of humor. She couldn't imagine how, though. He had to be in pain and terribly uncomfortable besides.

"I'm afraid I can't think of anything funny," Beth said, holding the hand he extended. "I know this is rough, Arnie, but I'm glad you're doing as well as you are."

He nodded. "Me, too. Fireball Roberts, Joe Weatherly, Tiny Lund, Grant Adcox, Neil Bonnett, Adam Petty, Dale Earnhardt—I could have joined them pretty easy. When you come as close as I did and don't go over, you wonder if God has some special purpose for you, something he wants you to do."

"Could be," she said. "When I say my prayers tonight I'll pray that he'll give you understanding of that special purpose, if there is one."

"You say your prayers?"

"Every night."

"Me, too."

Beth handed him a present, a bag of Golden Delicious apples. "An apple a day keeps the doctor away," she said.

"I wish you had given them to me before that darn race at Talladega," Arnie said. "I've seen more doctors than I knew existed."

He clenched his teeth as a pain stabbed in one of the many areas of his body that had been broken or bruised.

"Uh, we were talking about God," Arnie said. "I was brought up to go to church. Went to Oak Grove Baptist, a little country church at the foot of a mountain in St. Clair County. Mamma took me every time the doors opened. She's a good woman. I've always liked to go to church.

"She hates racing. She says even if it wasn't dangerous, it's not right to be doing it or going to see it on Sunday. That ain't keeping the Sabbath holy, she says, and it's hard to dispute that. She says when a driver gets hurt or killed, he isn't the only one who suffers. His family does, too. I can't dispute that, either. I guess she and Daddy have about wore out the hospital's chairs. And I know Mamma has about wore out God's ear praying for her boy.

"Daddy isn't against racing like she is, but after this experience he probably joins her in wishing I'd never climbed in a race car.

"I wonder if I should give it up. There's no denying the Bible says to honor your father and mother. Maybe that was what God was trying to tell me. What do you think, Beth?"

She gazed at the blank white wall of the hospital room. She remembered how she had disappointed her own mother by being a tomboy, by playing on the golf team at the University of Alabama, by becoming a sports writer. The Junior League, not the National Football League, was her mother's delight. She thought Beth should be helping plan a country club charity ball, not watching some idiot bat a ball.

And now, to make it even worse, Beth was covering stock car racing, a sport her mother ranked on the same level as dipping snuff and patronizing topless bars. All the drivers did wear leather jackets and ride motorcycles and look forward to their next visit to the tattoo parlor, didn't they?

But the comparison between her predicament and Arnie's was not exact. Her mother wanted to control her, to place her on exhibit in society, to have a daughter who was felicitous among what she considered the best people, a daughter who fit the proper definition of a lady. Beth wasn't going to get killed covering a ball game or race, but Arnie might well lose his life in his sport. Her mother's concerns for her were based on superficialities; Arnie's mother's concerns for him were based on very real dangers.

"I wish I could give you an answer," Beth told the race driver, "but I can't. I wish the pieces of life fit together ever so neatly, and there was a correct, one-sentence answer for every problem, but it's not that way.

"I will say this. If you quit racing I think it will leave a vacuum in your life that will never be filled. Some day you'd probably blame your mother because you never accomplished what you wanted to accomplish. But I can see this from her viewpoint, too, Arnie. I would be terrified if I had a nineteen-year-old son racing. And I would be distraught if he was seriously injured, as you have been.

"I think it has to be your decision whether you race or don't race, and I think you must be prepared to live with that decision. I don't know what you should do."

She recalled her fears when David Marlow crashed at Talladega, her panic when she feared his car was burning at Rockingham. She was so frightened she didn't even realize the man who was holding her was Herman Lanston. And look what her concern had gotten her: David thought she was Lanston's mistress.

Beth needed someone to talk to. She felt guilty for pouring her problems onto the injured Arnie Shale, but she told him all about the incident atop Lanston's truck, about the mysterious pictures that seemed to incriminate her, about David's calling her a spy for Lanston.

"He was here yesterday," Arnie said.

"Who?"

"David Marlow. He detoured on his way home to Daytona Beach from Rockingham. Flew his own plane straight to Birmingham just to see me. He told me to keep my chin up. You know, he's the only driver who has been to see me. Nobody else has even telephoned. He was sitting right there in that chair you're sitting in."

Beth found herself running her fingertips lightly over the arms of the chair, touching where David's arms had touched. "That sounds like something he would do," she said. "He's a good man. That's why I don't want to lose him. But I don't know what to do."

Arnie turned onto his side, facing her, and the pain triggered by the movement showed on his face. "If you were my girl I'd believe anything you said," he told her. "I would even believe you before I'd believe photographic evidence to the contrary. The camera could lie, but I'd know you wouldn't."

It was a marvelous remark, she thought. She remembered Arnie's asking her to go with him to the party at the mansion in Talladega, her saying she couldn't go and then showing up with Herman Lanston. She remembered Arnie's acceptance of her explanation and apology. Why couldn't David have that much faith in her?

She squeezed Arnie's arm and told him she'd like to interview him if he felt up to it. "I'd rather be talking to you than having those morons on TV talking to me," he said.

She hadn't filled a page of her notebook with notes before Arnie's mother entered the room. She frowned when she saw Beth. "So you're still at it, making my son into a hero to your readers?" she said. "Well, he doesn't look like a hero to me. He looks like a boy who is all beat up for no good reason. The next wreck might kill him, and if that happened your readers would forget all about him in a month."

The woman wouldn't have believed how strongly Beth respected her views, how intensely she empathized with her, so there was no need to say it. Cora Shale saw Beth as a functionary of racing, the sport—no, the insanity—that had almost killed her son. To Arnie's mother, Beth was the enemy.

"I'll go and leave you two alone," Cora Shale said. "I'll be in the cafeteria, son. I'll come back when this woman is finished with you."

"Mamma, don't . . ."

But Mrs. Shale closed the door and plodded down the hospital corridor, tired, bone weary.

BLAKE WATKINS STUDIED the Arnie Shale interview on the screen of his computer. Beth sat at her desk across the room. The sports editor's head nodded as he read, and she knew that was a good sign.

"Nice story," he said. "Understated, which is how I like such pieces. We'll string it across the top of the lead sports page in tomorrow's paper."

Beth was beaming—but her smile wavered when Watkins said, "There's something I've been meaning to mention to you."

"Something's wrong?"

"No, no, just the opposite. You've done such a good job that you've made me look smart by moving Charlie Murphy off the racing beat and you onto it. One of the publisher's friends is a big racing fan, and he told him how he liked your stuff, and the publisher told me, and I'm telling you.

"What I want you to think about is writing a weekly racing column, starting next season. We've never had one before, and it would be well read. The Auburn and Alabama beat men write columns, and so could you. You could state your views on what's happening on the racing scene, write lively opinion pieces, say what you think about the good, the bad, and the ugly."

Beth surged forward in her seat. If she had been in a cartoon, as Arnie

Shale had suggested he was, the illustrator would have drawn a light bulb being turned on above her head. "Blake, let me start writing that column now, this week," she said.

"Naw, let's wait until next season, at Daytona," he said. "Let's get you grounded in this sport a little more."

"Please, Blake, now."

"Naw, too early."

"Let's do this. Let me write a column I have in mind, and if you don't love it you can kill it. If you do love it, you run it as the first of my weekly columns."

"What is this subject that's so hot?" he asked.

"It's a secret. I'll tie up a few loose ends and send it from Phoenix, and you can run it Sunday."

"Or kill it," he said.

"You won't kill it."

"Well, I guess I can stand a little mystery in my life," the sports editor said. "Go to it."

BETH PARKED HER Miata in the parking deck at the Birmingham airport and tugged on two carry-ons that she had stuffed into the car's tiny trunk. She preferred not to check luggage because there was no telling where it would go. Apparently plenty of flyers shared her fears, because the overhead bins were always crammed full.

The next Winston Cup race was at Phoenix International Raceway. She had never been to Arizona, and she was looking forward to the change of scenery.

She passed the metal detectors, walked down the corridor to her gate, and got in line for a boarding pass. "Oh, good gosh, no," she whispered. "Of all people."

Ahead of her was Charlie Murphy. The new public relations man for the Penderton Tools racing team was flying to Phoenix, too.

Murphy got his boarding pass and joined a woman and two little girls who waited by a huge window that looked out onto the area in which a jet was being prepared for takeoff. He didn't notice Beth. Good.

Beth recognized the woman as Floreen Murphy, his wife, whom she had met at an office Christmas party. "All right," Floreen said, "you kids get over here by the windows and get your picture taken with Grandaddy."

Charlie spread an arm over the shoulders of each of the girls, who appeared to be about six and seven years old. The window framed the trio, and the jet was imposing in the background.

Floreen removed an expensive-looking camera from an expensive-looking leather case that hung by a strap around her neck. "Say cheese," she said, and she shot a picture. She admonished the children to be still and shot two more.

Then she handed the camera to Charlie, who commanded, "Say cheese," but quickly reached for one of the girls who was climbing over the back of a chair.

"I look awful, Charlie!" the woman yelled angrily. "Don't make my picture!" Charlie muttered something and put the camera back into its case, and the case into his carry-on luggage.

Suddenly it didn't take much imagination to envision Murphy pointing that same expensive camera at a horrified woman as she watched a car burn and clung to a man she didn't realize was Herman Lanston.

She hadn't thought of Murphy as a camera type. Certainly he didn't shoot his own pictures when he worked for the newspaper. But a camera probably would be handy equipment for a racing PR flack. And, what was most important to Charlie, he could put the purchase on an expense account.

Beth got her boarding pass and walked across the waiting room to where Murphy and the other three sat. He was tying the youngest girl's shoelace. "Charlie, you didn't even tell me to say cheese that day in Rockingham," Beth said.

Murphy looked up, so startled that he brushed the child's shoe off her foot. "Uh, hello, Miss Barrett," he mumbled. "Uh, this is my wife, Floreen, and my granddaughters Margaret and Heather. This is Beth Barrett. Miss Barrett works at the paper."

"We've met," Floreen said icily, and Beth knew Charlie had filled her head with stories of how an incompetent, conniving woman had stolen his job as racing writer of *The Birmingham News*. He wouldn't be above saying she had slept her way into it.

"We brought Granddaddy to the airport to have our picture made with him and an airplane," the oldest girl said. "I'm going to be a flight attendant when I get big, and I'll look at that picture and remember the day I decided to be one."

"I'm going to be a pilot and fly a plane just like that one," the youngest chimed in.

"That will be fun," Beth said. "Your granddaddy can make your pictures in your uniforms. He made some pictures of me one time."

Floreen turned to her husband with a quizzical expression that was the beginning of a glare. *Let him stew*, Beth thought.

"Can we see the pictures he made of you?" the oldest girl asked.

"You'll have to ask your granddaddy about that," she said. "Well, I've got a book I'm going to read while I wait for the plane. Nice to see you, Floreen. You, too, Margaret and Heather. See you on board, Charlie."

Beth read a few pages in a novel called *The Lost Sunshine*, about a newspaperman, but she couldn't concentrate for picturing in her mind Murphy snapping the photographs of her and Lanston. She had brought a copy of the photo with her, and when she studied it she reckoned he had shot it from atop another race car transporter.

She was glad when their flight was called, glad to join the hustle and bustle of boarding the plane and stuffing the overhead compartments. Her seat was near the back and Murphy's was near the front, both in coach. He glanced at her after he located his seat, but he quickly looked away.

Beth couldn't help but smile when she saw the expensive leather briefcase he carried. No doubt it was an expense account item, too. When he was at the newspaper he was famous for his filthy cloth briefcase that must have been a quarter-century old.

The plane lifted into the sky and headed west. An hour later Charlie Murphy walked down the aisle toward the bathroom at the rear of the craft. He gazed straight ahead, never looking her way.

Murphy wasn't finished with his mischief, Beth guessed. He'd pass out more of his damnable photographs in Phoenix.

Should she? Could she? She could. She heard the click of the bathroom door opening and closing, and she walked up the aisle, to Murphy's seat, trying to be quick about it but not be thought suspicious by the other passengers.

His briefcase lay in his aisle seat. "Hello," she said, smiling ever so pleasantly at the young couple in the middle and window seats. "Excuse me."

She popped the metal latches on the briefcase, thumbed through a sheaf of papers and saw what she was looking for—ten copies of the photo of her and Herman Lanston. She pulled out the photos, latched the briefcase, smiled at the couple, and returned to her seat, where she secreted the pictures in her own briefcase.

She had barely closed it when she heard the bathroom door open. Charlie Murphy ambled to his seat. He put his briefcase in an overhead compartment without looking inside.

The plane sped on, toward the sandy, jagged landscape of Arizona.

Chapter 15

*B*eth's mother frequently expounded on the essential triviality of her daughter's profession of sports writer. She delighted in using words that real people never use in conversation, and *puerile* was one of her favorites in this context.

How could it possibly matter which insane daredevil could drive an obnoxiously loud automobile around and around and around in a circle fastest? How could anyone remotely care which helmeted stranger could zig-zag best with a preposterously shaped ball under his arm? It was downright *jejune*.

But devoting a week to the selection of a gown to wear to a country club dance wasn't? Sometimes Beth deflected her mother's lecture by declaring that hitting a ball with a club was no more frivolous than attending a ball at the club.

Yet, Beth herself occasionally reflected on the curious nature of sports. Millions of fans spent a vast fortune each sports season to watch strangers perform feats that, in themselves, weren't significant. Indeed, what did throwing a ball into an iron hoop accomplish—even if the thrower was being paid millions of dollars a year?

The thought flitted across her mind as she gazed at Phoenix International Raceway for the first time. It was okay as speedways go, but viewed against the backdrop of God's own mountains it was a reminder of man's limitations. Its core was a mile of asphalt constructed for the purpose of determining the fastest driver. But didn't they just identify the fastest driver at a track in North Carolina? Why must it be done all over again? As some football player once said, "If the Super Bowl is the ultimate football game, why will they play it again next year?"

But, she knew, that was simply abstract musing. Nothing was meaningless if it had meaning to someone. Attending movies, listening to music on the radio, watching soap operas on television, playing dominoes, cheering for ballplayers and race drivers—those all help divert our thoughts from the grind of everyday life, cause us to forget momentarily that the spirit-numbing factory or office job and the tyrannical boss await on Monday.

So, she reminded herself, there was a purpose to her traveling all over the country to speedways of varying lengths and shapes and degrees of banking, to write about the coronation of each week's fastest man. The races relieved the tedium of fans' existence, and by writing about them, so did she. If it wasn't a noble calling, it was at least as important as teaching karate or ballet to kids.

Beth shuffled through the releases in the infield press room, looking for the points standings. She would help relieve that tedium by listing the standings in *The Birmingham News*, by creating an escapist story about a terrifically close points battle. She could picture her mother reading it and shaking her head in disdain at the notion that an arbitrary system of acquiring "points" would create a season's "champion."

The bins in the press room were stuffed with handouts. Flacks for manufacturers and teams supplied information about their clients, ranging from cliché quotes to thoughtful feature stories that reporters were welcome to plagiarize, cannibalize, or use to make paper airplanes, as long as the message was printed or broadcast.

She saw Charlie Murphy's flowery stuff on the Penderton Tools driver, a veteran named Shirley Portas who hadn't won a race in more than four years. She recalled Charlie laughing about a man being named Shirley when he wrote racing for the newspaper. "He couldn't outrun that other Shirley," he would add. "Shirley Temple, I mean." Now he was attempting to drum up publicity for Shirley Portas and Penderton Tools. Well, he wouldn't do it through her. She wouldn't mention either one in any of her articles. If Charlie Murphy was going to succeed as a racing flack, it would be without her assistance.

Beth found the points standings on a sheet of paper emblazoned with the NASCAR logo. David Marlow's victory and Vern Parchman's crash at Rockingham had shaken up the standings. With three races to go, Parchman led the second-place Marlow by just twelve points and the third-place Raider Slater by thirty-nine points.

Beth studied her record book and learned that the narrowest points victory in the history of the series occurred in 1992. Alan Kulwicki beat out Bill Elliott for the title by a mere ten points, 4,078 to 4,068. Davey Allison was third with 4,015.

With three races to go in 1992, Elliott led Allison by thirty-nine points and Kulwicki by forty-seven. With two races to go, Elliott led Allison by seventy points and Kulwicki by eighty-five. With one race to go, Allison led Kulwicki by thirty points and Elliot by forty.

The final race was a five-hundred-miler at Atlanta. Alabama racing fans were solidly behind Davey Allison, the son and Hueytown neighbor of the great Bobby Allison. They might not recall all the details, but they still remember the drama and the numbing disappointment of the event.

Davey could lock up the championship by finishing sixth or better. With just 43 of the 328 laps remaining, he was, indeed, in sixth place and advancing toward the front. But a tire on another driver's car went down, and that driver lost control and knocked Allison out of the race.

Elliott drove to victory at Atlanta, but Kulwicki finished second and won the championship by ten points. Kulwicki received the five-point bonus for leading more laps than anyone else. He was in front 103 times to Elliott's 102.

If Elliott had led one more lap and Kulwicki one fewer, Elliott would have received the five-point bonus, and they would have finished in a tie in the season's points. Elliott would have been declared the champion because he won more races than Kulwicki. Bill was victorious five times, Alan twice.

The drama of that race wasn't limited to the points chase. Richard Petty, the sport's winningest driver with two hundred victories, was retiring, competing in his final event.

Before a third of the race had unfolded, Petty was involved in an accident that caused a fire under the hood of his car. His crew worked hard to restore it to running order, and with a lap remaining, Petty returned to the track and finished his career in motion.

There was another aspect of that race that was dramatic in retrospect. It was the first Cup event for another driver. Magnificent Jeff Gordon made his debut in the event in which magnificent Richard Petty ended his career.

Beth wondered how she could stuff all that information into the fifteen column inches Blake Watkins wanted her to write for the next morning's editions. Watkins hated long stories, said the mere sight of them scared off readers, who were in a hurry to have their minds and morals corrupted by some imbecilic television show. Watkins despised TV, said its trashy programs had done more to rip the fabric of America than anything else, and he delighted in beating the television boys and girls on news stories.

Beth knew, too, that she would have to devote at least a paragraph to the sad fate of two of the principals in that 1992 points battle. Alan Kulwicki and Davey Allison lost their lives in crashes—not racing wrecks but aircraft accidents. Talk about the vagaries of life.

They were professionals pitching themselves full-bore into the battle for the 1992 championship, and now they were gone. Vern Parchman,

David Marlow, and Raider Slater were professionals pitching themselves full-bore into the current points battle, and what if . . .

Her research into 1992 had intrigued her at first, but now she was gloomy and she needed to clear her mind. She went outside the infield press room and breathed the dry Arizona air. She regarded the mountains on the horizon, wondered how many millions of years they had existed, and reflected that the world kept spinning, no matter what. She scanned a cactus-dotted hillside that would accommodate hardy fans who would spread blankets and eat picnic lunches on race day. Yes, people needed relief from the slings and arrows of life, and they might as well find it at a race track as at a country club.

She dreaded that first stroll through the garage area, dreaded getting the cold shoulder from David Marlow and Pappy Draper, but it couldn't be avoided. A reporter had to reconnoiter the scene at every track, to alert herself to any changes, such as one driver's name disappearing from a car and another's replacing it.

David wasn't in the team's garage stall, but Pappy was. He was lecturing a young crewman, making motions with both hands, illustrating something mechanical. He glanced over the crewman's shoulder and saw Beth. He hesitated for a moment, then his eyes returned to the crewman and he resumed his instructions.

That hurt. Beth fixed her eyes on the mountains and continued her walk. She acknowledged driver Brad Statham's cheery "hi there" with a forced smile and barely perceptible nod.

A voice behind her said, "I'm going to have to get me one of them Dutch boy haircuts. Maybe then Brad Statham would give me a tumble."

Beth knew the voice belonged to Margie Swangler, a legendary public relations rep for veteran driver Whitey Middlesworth's team.

Margie had graciously helped Beth become acclimated to the racing beat. Beth stopped and gave her a hug. "You can have my haircut, honey," Beth said. "It isn't doing anything for my love life these days."

Margie Swangler was a character, a throwback to the old free-wheeling days of stock car racing. She had grown up in it. Her daddy owned a quarter-mile bullring in South Carolina, and as a kid she did whatever was needed, from taking tickets to selling hot dogs to sweeping up. As a high schooler she wrote racing advances and results and charmed the local daily newspaper's anti-racing editor into running them. "I say charmed; some say blackmailed," she told the story, with an accompanying snort of a laugh. "Old boy just couldn't keep his hands to himself."

She married an English teacher and left him eight months later. She married a dirt-track driver and bailed out on him in seven months. She didn't bother with such technicalities as divorces.

For three seasons she drove a Modified race car at her daddy's track, competing against the men. She never won. She finished second once, and when she noticed the car in Victory Lane was equipped with illegal tires, she demanded her daddy disqualify the winner. He said he couldn't take a victory away from the fellow and hand it to his daughter, even if he was cheating. It would be terrible PR. So she got a screwdriver and punctured all four of the winner's tires. She dared him to do anything about it. He noted the .38 revolver in her non-screwdriver hand and decided not to protest.

A friend of her daddy, remembering her knack for getting stories in the paper when she was a girl, hired her to be the flack for his Winston Cup team, and she had been tub-thumping for various big league teams for twenty-six years, the last fourteen for Chamblin Furniture's. Whitey Middlesworth had won a grand total of three races in his dozen years with the team, but he and Margie and Doc Chamblin, the owner, loved racing and got along well together, so they soldiered on. The influx of big money into the sport was strangling the team, though, and Middlesworth routinely failed to qualify for a third of the races.

The sixty-one-year-old Margie always wore a lavender cap and lavender satin jacket, no matter how hot the day. It was Chamblin

Furniture Racing's color, and she wanted to be easily identified.

"How goes it, girl?"

"Not good," Beth said.

"Yeah, I heard you and old scarface weren't getting along so well. Ain't nothing secret on the racing scene. Everybody loves to gossip."

"Margie, for goodness sake, don't call him that," Beth said. "That tiny scar on David's cheek is interesting, not ugly."

Margie laughed so hard she lapsed into a coughing spell. "I know it, I know it. I just wanted to see if you still loved the boy, and it's obvious you do."

"I suppose you saw the notorious photograph of Herman Lanston and me?" Beth said.

"I did. Also heard your explanation. I fancy myself a good judge of folks, and I believe you."

"Thanks," Beth said.

"Well, I'm going over and give Pappy Draper his good-luck hug. I do it at every stop on the circuit. He said it brings him good luck, that he'd hate to think what might happen if he didn't get his hug.

"I tell him I'm glad it brings him luck, 'cause it don't do nothing for me. Our poor old team couldn't win a race if we were on a motorcycle and the rest were on roller skates."

An idea struck Beth with the force of a revving race car motor. "You just walk up and give him a regular hug?" she asked Margie.

"That's it. I give him a good squeeze and sometimes a little peck on the cheek."

"Mind if I do it for you this time?" Beth asked.

"Naw, I don't mind," Margie said. "I don't exactly regard it as one of the great perks of the job."

"Let me borrow your cap and jacket."

"You been inhaling too much carbon monoxide," the older woman said. "They ain't what you'd call high fashion. But go ahead. Here."

Beth slipped on the lavender baseball-type cap and satin jacket, pulling the bill low on her forehead. She chose a moment when Draper was bent over a work bench. She approached from the rear, put her right arm around his shoulders and her left arm across his chest. She pressed the top of her head against his cheek.

Draper glimpsed the lavender jacket sleeve and the cap and said, "Margie, you old warhorse, you would have to grab me when I'm trying to solder this wire and can't plant a good smooch on you."

Beth remained silent and hugged him tighter.

"Now that ain't a hug," he said. "That's a downright embrace. I'll be so lucky now we'll win the race by five laps."

Silence.

"How's Whitey doing?" Pappy asked. "Is he keeping his spirits up? He ran a little better at Rockingham. I hope he can qualify here. Arizona's a long tow to not even make the field. I hurt for you guys."

Silence.

Pappy adjusted his reading glasses with the forefinger of his left hand, placed the soldering iron on the workbench, inspected his handiwork, and pronounced, "Perfecto!"

Smiling, he turned toward Beth and said, "What's the matter, Swangler? Cat got your . . . Why, Beth, what in the world?"

She said, "Isn't it amazing, Pappy, how someone can be hugging you and you don't even realize who the person is?"

"Uh, I guess so, but . . ."

Beth didn't let him finish. "I hope no one snapped a picture of us," she said. "If your wife saw it she might not believe you thought I was your old pal Margie Swangler. We don't look at all alike. Anyway, good luck, Pappy. Or at least I hope that hug will bring you good luck."

IT WAS SATURDAY morning, and Beth put the finishing touches on the first of her weekly racing columns, opinion pieces that would run in Sunday editions. She transmitted it over the telephone from her computer to the computer at *The Birmingham News.*

At least she *hoped* Blake Watkins would run it. She couldn't imagine that he wouldn't, for one of his favorite words described it.

Ten minutes later Watkins phoned her and, indeed, pronounced the article a "zinger." Not only would it run in that Sunday's paper, she was to continue to write a weekly column.

The column began:

> At Rockingham last Sunday, a car owner radioed these words to his driver as another driver attempted to pass: "Put him in the wall!"
>
> His driver replied: "You're crazy, Herman. Man, don't you know this ain't exactly a private conversation we're having?"
>
> The car owner is Herman Lanston, his driver is Vern Parchman, and the man who was passing Parchman is David Marlow, who used to drive for the Lanston Farms team.
>
> The radios that enable drivers and crew to communicate are a blessing, but they also can be a curse, for thousands of strangers can listen in on conversations that are meant to be private.

Beth wrote that behavior such as Lanston's was a detriment to racing, that it reinforced the opinion of many that the sport was inhabited by maniacs and watched by spectators who want to see someone killed. She said NASCAR should have fined Lanston or barred him from the pits and the garage area for a race or two, not merely reprimanded him.

She discussed the "mysterious" split between Lanston and Marlow without violating David's off-the-record edict.

By his order to Parchman to wreck a competitor, Lanston had disrespected the sport, the fans, and Marlow. She smiled as she wrote the concluding line:

Herman Lanston should not only apologize to David Marlow in person, he should issue a written apology to the fans who pay good money to see a clean sporting event.

THE STEAMING points battle was relegated to the back burner at Phoenix by a race that featured not Vern Parchman, David Marlow, and Raider Slater, but a couple of drivers named Brandon Templin and Hurston Mathes.

Templin had won two races in his long career, none in his last 223 starts. Mathes was winless in his four seasons on the circuit.

Both their teams hit on the elusive "combination" at Phoenix, though, and they staged a rousing storybook duel all day long. They crossed the line side by side on the final lap and the photo-finish camera was consulted to settle the issue. It showed that, by a margin of inches, Templin's losing streak had reached 224 races and Mathes was a victor for the first time.

Parchman never led a lap and finished ninth. Marlow led the first seventeen laps, but his car faded and he finished eleventh. Slater never got in front, and he finished seventh. For the second straight week, Shirley Portas required a relief driver before the race was two-thirds completed, causing his flack, Charlie Murphy, to duck into a bathroom for a pull at a pint of vodka.

After Phoenix, Parchman led Marlow by fifteen points and Slater by thirty-one.

The post-race press conference was a hoot as the exuberant Hurston

Mathes held court as wittily and satirically as Darrell Waltrip at
his best.

Beth knew she had a wonderful story on her hands, but what was
more wonderful to her was the visit to the press box by Pappy Draper
after Mathes had left and the other reporters were beginning their stories.

"Beth, I'm sorry I didn't trust you," he said. "I should have known
better. I consider myself a good judge of character, and I should have
stuck with my first appraisal of yours. I'll do my best to convince David
that photo is meaningless."

Beth patted his hand and said thanks, whereupon Pappy grinned and
added, "But you aren't near the good-luck hugger Margie Swangler is.
We couldn't outrun a snail today."

Chapter 16

Beth would give the public relations woman for a Birmingham clothing manufacturing company an "A" for not beating around the bush.

"Our CEO is a racing fan," the woman said into the telephone. "He would like to fly Arnie Shale to the race in Miami on our company jet. He would appreciate it if you would let your readers know about our wonderful kindness and generosity."

Beth answered her cynical chuckle with one of her own, but she asked the woman for the details and said she'd have a photographer at the airport to shoot the injured driver being loaded aboard the plane.

And she was pleased for Arnie. He'd had a hardscrabble racing career, but now he would receive the royal treatment, watching the race in a luxury box, eating shrimp and filet mignon. It was a shame, though, that his body had to be broken like saltine crackers that fell from a grocery cart for this benefactor to acquire an interest in him. The company could have given him thousands of dollars in sponsorship money when he was healthy, and never missed it.

But, hey, it was no small thing to be escaping the unseasonably cold weather by zooming off to Miami. Some Northerners mistakenly pictured Alabama as a land of perpetual summer, but there were many days in which nose-diving temperatures and whistling winds blurred the distinction between the state known as the Heart of Dixie and, say, Indiana. This November, in particular, had slandered the cliché of the sunny South, chilling the state's fanatical football fans to the bone as they packed stadiums in Auburn and Tuscaloosa and Birmingham.

Beth felt a surge of energy as she strode from the Miami International Airport terminal in the warmth of South Florida. She rented a car, pointed it south, and in half an hour she was admiring Homestead-Miami Speedway, site of the next to last race of the season, a four-hundred-miler that would be vitally important in determining the Winston Cup championship.

Its art deco architecture and vibrant colors gave it an appeal most speedways lacked. She had read that more than eight hundred palm trees dotted the property, and that didn't appear to be an exaggeration.

Beth signed for her credentials, visited the press box and the infield press room, and strolled through the garage area. There was Arnie Shale, in a wheelchair, surrounded by a corps of identically shirted inner-city kids who were the guests of another company that, no doubt, also wanted its wonderful kindness and generosity publicized. Arnie was signing autographs and recounting the story of his crash to wide-eyed children who tentatively touched the casts on his arm and leg.

"I've got an idea," he said when he signed the last autograph. "Why don't you all sign my casts? Get in line, now—one line for the leg and one for the arm. Got another pen, Ms. Harrison?"

The PR woman who had phoned Beth beamed and produced a second felt-tip pen, and the kids flew into action, writing their names in scripts of various heights and widths on the casts.

Beth had never met Ms. Harrison, but the young PR rep waved at her and said, "Ms. Barrett! I recognized you from the photo that ran with your column Sunday. Thank you for the nice article about us flying Arnie to Miami. I've been pushing him around the garage area. He has enjoyed seeing his friends, and he's wonderful with kids."

"He's quite a fellow," Beth said. "He would make a grand representative for your company if it ever decided to sponsor a race car." Might as well get to the core of the matter with Ms. Harrison, Beth thought. "What a national story it would be, how your kind and generous company flew Arnie to Miami out of the goodness of its heart and then was so impressed with the way he related to kids that it decided to sponsor him next season when he's well. It could be your idea. I'll bet your CEO would be impressed."

Ms. Harrison smiled knowingly. "It is a wonderful idea," she said. "But I would change one thing in the scenario. I would be sure it was my CEO's idea, not mine."

Beth laughed. She liked the woman. Ms. Harrison would go far. "I'll push Arnie's wheelchair and you can take a break," Beth said.

She wanted to chat with Arnie anyway. "Well, you're back in your element, the race track," she said.

"Yep. It feels good. I wish I had a faster vehicle, though, one I could drive myself and didn't have to rely on somebody to push me."

"Sorry, but this one-horsepower job is all that's available," Beth said.

"You're prettier than any horse I ever saw," Arnie said, "even a Kentucky Derby winner."

A couple of crewmen came over and shook Arnie's hand. "The *St. Clair County Special* is back!" one said. But the mechanics' chatter and laughter were forced, because they obviously didn't know whether the *St. Clair County Special* would ever be back. Not only was its driver seriously injured, but the face of racing was changing, and the shoestring operators were being forced out by the rich teams.

"I've decided one thing today," Arnie told Beth as she pushed his wheelchair through the garage area. "This is where I belong, where I want to be. I'm sorry to disappoint my mother, but it's my life, and I have to live it on my terms. I'm a race driver, and I'm going to race."

She knew those words would invoke terror and despair in his mother's heart, and Beth could hurt for her, but she also admired Arnie for living his own life. She had had to take a similar stand in the face of her mother's criticisms.

She continued to push Arnie, and drivers, mechanics, and reporters wished him well. Beth was startled when Arnie yelped, "Hey, there's Mr. Lanston standing at that transporter! Take me over there! I want to ask him if he was impressed with my run at Talladega."

Beth froze. The last person on earth she wanted to see was Herman Lanston, but how could she tell Arnie she wouldn't push him to where the car owner stood?

She didn't have to. Lanston spotted her and began walking double-time in her direction. His eyes were narrowed, his lips trembling in anger.

"Mr. Lanston!" Arnie said. "It's Arnie Shale! How did you like my charge at Talladega? Before the wreck, I mean. You said I might drive for you someday, and . . ."

Lanston glared at Arnie for a moment, as if he might be an intrusive insect, and then he turned the full force of his malevolence on Beth and yelled, "You bitch! I read that column! How dare you! If you ever write crap like that about me again I'll see that you end up in worse condition than this rube! A broken leg and a broken arm will seem like a scratch when my men get through with you!"

Mechanics put down their tools and stuck their heads out of their garage stalls to watch and listen. Beth couldn't help swallowing hard, but she forced herself to maintain eye contact with the ranting man. Lanston doubled his right fist and she feared he was actually going to slug her, but she didn't move.

"Now, just a minute," Arnie said, pain showing on his face as he leaned forward in the wheelchair. "You can't talk to her like that."

"Shut up, you pathetic idiot!" Lanston said. "I wouldn't let a country hick like you change a tire on my race car, much less drive it. Do you think I'm so dumb I don't know you had a hand grenade in that piece of junk at Talladega?"

A crowd was gathering. Lanston opened his mouth to say more, but instead he took a deep breath and walked away.

Beth reached into her jacket pocket and felt the soft vibration of her little tape recorder. "Well, I guess I've got my column subject for Sunday," she told Arnie.

A car owner threatening a reporter with bodily harm because she had written the truth, and cursing a broken young driver because he had spoken up in her defense—and all of it on tape. Blake Watkins would have his "zinger" for the second straight week.

"Beth."

Her name was spoken softly, in a tone she had heard years ago, when she was a college girl dating a dirt-track driver who didn't have enough money to buy movie tickets. It was the tone she had heard when she had dinner in Rockingham with a star of stock car racing's big league.

David Marlow stood behind her, and his lips moved as if he wanted to say more, but he turned and walked away.

She knew he had read or heard about her column criticizing Herman Lanston. She knew he had observed her encounter with Lanston seconds before. But he was simply too obstinate, too close-minded on the subject of Lanston to disregard the infamous photograph.

"Blockhead," she muttered.

"He's every bit of that," agreed Arnie Shale.

Beth smiled. Arnie was talking about Herman Lanston; she was talking about David Marlow.

Her adrenalin was bubbling after the run-in with Lanston, and it fueled her for a showdown with Charlie Murphy. She didn't know what she'd say to Murphy, but she'd say something, and now was the time to say it. She returned Arnie and his wheelchair to Ms. Harrison and began searching out the Penderton Tools flack.

She spotted Murphy in the company of a reporter from Nashville. She knew they were old friends. Murphy was gesturing wildly, raising his arms in a sign of perplexed despair. She joined them.

"Hi, Beth," the reporter said. "Good column on Herman Lanston."

Murphy glared at her, obviously waiting for her to leave so he could continue his tirade. She didn't.

A few seconds of silence followed, then the reporter asked, "Why can't Portas finish a race, Charlie?"

"Because he's a fat, beer-swilling, unmotivated piece of crap who never has a thought beyond himself," Murphy said. He was on a roll, too angry to be discreet in the presence of the woman he despised. "What do you expect from a man named Shirley?"

"But why are you so upset?" the reporter asked. "They don't expect you to drive the car, do they?"

"Hell, no," Murphy roared, "but they expect me to publicize the one who does. Old Alex Penderton says having a driver named Shirley ought to be a plus. He said Johnny Cash used to sing about boy named Sue, and if I'd do my job, folks would be writing about a boy named Shirley.

"Hell, how can you expect reporters to write about somebody who can't finish a race. Shirley has had to have a relief driver the last two shows. Nobody wants to write about a slob who can't even go the route. Besides, the Shirley angle was done to death years ago. Alex Penderton doesn't have a clue about publicity—or much of anything else, judging from the way this team operates."

Beth knew an opportunity when she saw it. "If you're so miserable, Charlie, maybe you should get back into sports writing," she said in a friendly tone.

Murphy exploded, as she knew he would. "I'd be in the newspaper business now if you hadn't stolen my job!"

"As I recall, I had a job and you had a job, and I kept mine and you resigned yours," she said sweetly.

"You know what the hell I mean!' Murphy raved.

"So you think Alex Penderton doesn't have a clue?" Beth said.

The question waved a caution flag in his mind, and Murphy put the brakes to his diatribe. "Now, what we've talked about here is off the record," he said.

"You didn't mention off the record," Beth reminded, "so that makes it on the record. You're a legitimate spokesman for a big league racing team."

Suddenly this man who hated her, this man who told David Marlow she was one of Herman Lanston's chippies, this man who shot and then misrepresented a photograph of her and Lanston—this man was patting her on the shoulder and saying, "Now, honey, I need this job. You wouldn't . . ."

"Honey, you'd better believe I would," Beth said.

"My word against yours," Charlie said. "Old Gordon here wouldn't have any reason to get involved."

Again, Beth felt the vibration of her recorder in her jacket pocket. "I wouldn't need old Gordon," she said. "I've got it on tape."

Murphy grabbed at the recorder but Beth anticipated the move. She stepped back and held it behind her. "Charlie, don't do anything stupid," said Gordon, the reporter from Nashville.

"What do you want?" Murphy asked her.

"First, I want Gordon to give us a minute of privacy," she said.

"I'm gone," Gordon said. "Gladly."

They watched the reporter walk away, then Charlie said, "This is dirty pool, girl."

"I'm not a girl. I'm a woman. And I'll bow to your judgment, because you should recognize dirty pool if anyone does."

"So, what do you what?"

"I want you to go to David Marlow and tell him you lied about my being one of Lanston's girls. I want you to tell him I thought his car was on fire at Rockingham, and I wasn't aware I was on Lanston's transporter or that it was Lanston I was hugging. I want you to tell him I pulled away when I realized it was Lanston. I want you to tell him you shot rapid-fire photos and picked the most incriminating one because you hate me because Blake Watkins assigned me to the racing beat."

"I can't do that," Murphy sputtered. "Marlow and I have always gotten along, and he'll despise me."

"Then read about yourself in my column Sunday," Beth said.

"All right, all right, I'll do it," Murphy said. "I'm on my way."

"I'm going with you," Beth said.

Murphy shook his head but then said, "Okay, okay."

Beth walked behind him as he headed for David Marlow's garage stall. She kissed her tape recorder. "Sweet little thing," she whispered. "You came through twice today."

"What?" Charlie said.

"Nothing. Keep moving."

When they reached David's garage stall he was overseeing the adjustment of the safety harness in his car. Murphy asked him to step outside into the warm Florida sunshine. Then he confessed his sins, as if he were talking to a priest instead of a race driver.

"I'm sorry I did it," Charlie said, "and I apologize to both of you."

"Oh, Charlie, you're just sorry you got caught," Beth said.

David told Murphy to get out of his sight and never speak to him again. He took Beth in his arms and kissed her on the lips. So what if a dozen crewmen were watching? "I'm sorry, too," he told her. "I'm sorry I let my loathing of Herman Lanston cloud my judgment to the point I almost lost you. I was a, er, er . . ."

"A blockhead?" she offered.

"Yep, a real blockhead," he said.

HURSTON MATHES WON at Phoenix, and Hurston Mathes was leading at Homestead-Miami. Sometimes it happened like this, a writer told Beth. A driver goes for years without a victory, and then he wins his first race, and that serves as a breakthrough, and he becomes a regular winner.

Perhaps that first visit to Victory Lane instills confidence that was lacking in driver and crew. Maybe they just become more serious about the task at hand. Since racers are devoutly superstitious, maybe the driver wore a pair of new gold socks when he scored his first victory, and maybe now he's wearing them every week.

In any event, Hurston Mathes—who hadn't won in four years on the circuit—was pursuing his second straight victory. With 228 laps completed and 39 trips around the mile-and-a-half track remaining, he was four hundred yards ahead of David Marlow. He had dominated the race, leading all but a handful of laps.

Suddenly an eruption of white smoke from under the hood of his car signaled the end of Hurston Mathes's day. His motor couldn't answer the demands he had made of it.

"Told you," Marlow said into his radio. "To finish first, you must first finish."

"You were right," Pappy Draper answered, "but you had me scared there for awhile."

Marlow had read accounts of the overdone, theatrical press conference that followed Mathes's victory at Rockingham and suspected the young driver would be so full of himself in the next race that he would attempt a runaway, that he would overextend his equipment. David told the crew chief he planned to hang back, save his car, and let Mathes go. "I'll bet you a steak he doesn't complete the race," Marlow had said.

Pappy approved the strategy, but as the laps wound down he became increasingly edgy. At one point Mathe was a mere three hundred yards shy of lapping David, Vern Parchman, and Raider Slater, who were running in a tight pack of three. He had lapped everyone else. But a caution flag enabled the trio to catch back up.

"Let's don't get so carried away with our brilliant strategy that we lose the confounded race," Pappy had blurted when Mathes threatened to lap David.

"Have faith," David calmly counseled.

Beth eavesdropped on their conversations and reckoned that since David was laying back, his car must be considerably stronger than Parchman's and Slater's. But she was disappointed to hear David tell Pappy that the strategies of the other two were identical to his—they were biding their time, waiting for Mathes's racer to fail, and then they would join David in a three-man shootout at the end. Nobody had to tell Marlow that; experience told him.

Mathes's dying motor dropped oil on the track, and most of the cars took advantage of the resulting caution period to pit for four tires and a load of fuel. All could go the distance.

Thanks to fast work by Pappy Draper and the crew, David was in the lead when the race resumed under green. Slater was second, Parchman third. "You're in command, boy," said Draper. "They've got to take it away from you."

"The only thing that bothers me, Pappy, is that Parchman might have been hanging back even more than Slater and I were. He might have us both covered."

"Damn," said Pappy, "his crew chief is grinning at me right now."

"You've been around too long to fall for that," David said. "It's just psychology. He figured you'd tell me—and you did."

"Sorry," Pappy said. "You're probably right."

David's voice was even—assertive but even—as he said, "I'm going to win this race, Pappy. And I'm going to win this championship."

Beth felt a surge of exhilaration. For the first time, she was covering a race from the infield press room—watching it on TV mostly—and when David won the race she could rush to Victory Lane, press her face to the fence, and watch her man receive his recognition.

Marlow extended his lead over Slater to fifty yards, and Parchman seemed content to hang another fifty yards behind Slater.

A man who had been invisible most of the day was charging into the picture. Brad Statham took fourth place, and then he was on Parchman's bumper.

Beth tuned in Parchman on her scanner and heard Herman Lanston yell, "Ten laps to go, Vern! Make your move!"

But Statham intruded the front quarter panel of his car beside the rear quarter panel of Parchman's on the outside, and Parchman's car wiggled in the disturbed air. It moved up the track, almost taking both of them out.

The bobble cost Parchman time, and Slater increased the distance between his car and Parchman's.

Statham tried to go low but Parchman cut him off, and again Parchman's racer got out of shape. "It's pushing!" Parchman said. "That and Statham's chopping up the air."

Beth tuned in David's frequency in time to hear him say, "It's running like a dream, Pappy. I'm stretching my lead over Slater every lap. What's happening to Parchman?"

"Brad Statham is racing him, and that's letting you and Slater get away. Brad's battling him for third place like it's for the win. Parchman is having to concentrate on holding him off."

Slater was the slice of ham in an expanding sandwich. As the laps wound down, Marlow increased his lead over Raider and Parchman fell farther behind Raider.

"That idiot Statham!" Lanston screamed. "We've got a championship to win, and he's messing us up! NASCAR should black-flag him!"

Frustration and anger were mixed in Parchman's voice: "He's just doing his job, Herman. He's a racer and he's racing."

Marlow crossed the finish line uncontested and Slater wasn't pressed for second place. Statham passed Parchman in the fourth turn of the final lap and finished third.

"Way to go, Brad," Beth whispered, for she knew that meant Marlow and Parchman would enter the final race of the season, at Atlanta, tied for the lead in the standings. Slater would be but twenty-one points behind them.

She was happy for David, but she was happy for Brad Statham, too. Herman Lanston also had stabbed him in the back years ago, and she knew he was delighted not only to outrun Parchman but to damage his chances at the championship.

She stood outside Victory Lane and watched as David contorted himself from the car and sprayed champagne on his helpless subjects. He thanked half the companies on earth for the contribution to his victory.

Then, in all the melee, he spotted her through the fence. He said something to an official, and the man unlocked the gate and invited her inside.

There, before millions on national television, David Marlow planted a big, champagne-wet kiss on Beth Barrett's lips.

Chapter 17

*T*he business writer of *The Birmingham News* handed Beth Barrett a printout of an Associated Press story and said, "This could have a major effect on racing, couldn't it?"

Indeed. The story said Lanston Farms had bought Bibley Designs. The multi-million-dollar deal would be the first in a series of acquisitions in the spirit of what Herman Lanston called "a new philosophy of diversification."

To her it meant one thing: Vern Parchman's sponsor had bought David Marlow's sponsor and would have control of both racing teams, as the drivers—who were tied at the top of the points standings— approached the final race of the season at Atlanta Motor Speedway.

She had barely digested the story when she received a phone call from a Lanston Farms PR man notifying her that Herman Lanston had called a press teleconference to discuss the racing ramifications of the purchase. He gave her the access phone number and said goodbye, never mentioning the second "zinger" column she had written about Lanston, in which she quoted him as insulting Arnie Shale and threatening to have her injured.

Beth read the AP story again. She didn't understand all the business terms but she understood one thing: Herman Lanston was buying

Bibley Designs simply to acquire its racing team. What other reason could there be? Why else would Lanston Farms buy this particular company at this particular time? Lanston would stop at nothing to win the championship.

She passed the information on to Blake Watkins. "Listen in on the teleconference and ask some questions," the sports editor said. "Keep calm. Don't get in a yelling match with Lanston. We'll see what we've got when it's over."

Racing writers from across the nation dialed into the teleconference. Lanston greeted them with excessive cordiality. "Fred, how's the new baby? Mickey, congratulations on winning that writing award. Ralph, I noticed your alma mater's football team won again. Beth, it's nice to hear your voice."

She wanted to throw up.

He explained that Lanston Farms' purchase of Bibley Designs was purely a business decision. It had nothing to do with racing. It was a coincidence that Lanston Farms' driver and Bibley Designs' driver were in a monumental battle for the championship.

He would field two cars at Atlanta, both under the Lanston Farms banner and carrying the Lanston Farms colors. Vern Parchman would drive one, David Marlow the other.

"The cars will be as equal as we can get them, and may the best man win."

Now Beth really wanted to throw up.

When one company acquires another, it sometimes "streamlines," Lanston said. It sees ways to cut costs and make the operation more efficient that might not have been visible to the former owners. Some two hundred employees of Bibley Designs would be terminated—including all the personnel of the racing team. Except, of course, David Marlow.

"We have a Lanston Farms crew that is perfectly capable of fielding two cars for one race," he explained. "All of the employees of the former Bibley Designs racing team will receive nice severance checks in recognition of their service."

The reporters were invited to ask questions, and they had plenty of them.

What was to keep Lanston from assigning David Marlow to an inferior car, thereby assuring Parchman would win the championship?

"My integrity," Lanston answered. "And consider this. You are assuming I prefer that Parchman wins, but you haven't considered that Parchman is retiring after this season and Marlow might be my driver next year, so perhaps it would be advantageous for me to start next season with the defending champion driving for Lanston Farms. Of course, that's all academic, because I intend to give both drivers strong cars at Atlanta and let the chips fall where they may."

Would Marlow, indeed, drive Lanston's car at Atlanta?

"I haven't talked to him, but I assume he will," Lanston said. "I now hold his contract. I can't think of any reason he would not drive it."

But Marlow once walked out on Lanston in the middle of a season. Why?

"Oh, that's ancient history," Lanston said. "I have no animosity toward David Marlow, and I hope he has none against me. I think he would be a most deserving champion, and I would be as proud if he drove my car to the title as I would be if Parchman won it."

Beth covered the mouthpiece of her telephone and told Blake Watkins, "The bullstuff is about knee deep. You may have to shovel me out."

A reporter from Philadelphia changed the subject. He asked Lanston how he felt about the columns Beth had written about him on two successive Sundays.

Lanston was prepared. "I'm a competitor," he said. "I don't like to lose, and sometimes that leads me to speak when I shouldn't, to say things I don't mean. Certainly I wouldn't condone my driver wrecking another man. Certainly I wouldn't cause Miss Barrett or any other person any harm. Certainly I don't know anyone who would injure anyone else on my orders. Maybe I've watched *The Godfather* too many times.

Certainly I have nothing but the highest regard for Arnie Shale, as a driver and as a person. I want to apologize to Miss Barrett, to Mr. Shale, to the fans for my being a blabbermouth. I consider she has done me a service by pointing out my shortcomings, and I will correct them."

Beth covered the mouthpiece again and told Watkins, "Now the bullstuff is waist deep."

She identified herself to the moderator and asked Lanston when he planned to discuss the change with Marlow.

"I'm not sure, Beth," he answered in a friendly tone. "As you can imagine, I'm extremely busy working on the many aspects of this deal, apart from the racing questions."

Beth knew the writers would try to contact David as soon as Lanston's teleconference ended. As the reporters ran out of questions, she wrote David's home phone number on a piece of paper and handed it to a copy boy. "Call him and tell him to hold until I get to the telephone," she said.

Two questions later, Lanston signed off. Beth took the other phone and greeted David. "Hello, Dutch Boy," he said.

He hadn't heard the news. Beth read part of the story to him and told him about Lanston's press conference. He was silent for a moment as he tried to sort out the implications. "Buying my racing team is radical even for that rattlesnake," he said.

"Oh, David, he's going to cheat you out of the championship." Beth said.

"That's what he's planning," David said. "He'd put me in a car that would go fast but that wouldn't last five hundred miles. Of course I won't drive for him. I'd just sit out the race and lose the championship before I'd let him do that to me."

"I need a quote for my story, Darling," she said, "and all the other reporters will be calling you."

"Just quote me as saying I have no comment. I won't answer this line again, but you can always reach me on my cell phone. I'll tell the team's

PR man to issue a statement saying I have no comment if he hasn't cleaned out his desk and vamoosed.

"I'm glad there's an off-week before the final race. I'm going to swim in the ocean and relax on the beach for a couple of days. I'll try to determine what my options are."

THE NEXT DAY Arnie Shale phoned Beth and asked her to lunch. He suggested they meet at 1:30 in his hometown of Springville at a cafe that specialized in country cooking. Most of the customers would be gone by then. One of his volunteer crew members would transport him and his wheelchair and come back for him an hour later.

Beth drove the thirty miles from downtown Birmingham. When she arrived at the cafe a couple of fans were patting the local hero on the back and asking when he would return to racing, but they cleared out and she and Arnie were alone.

"I read your story in this morning's paper," Arnie began. "I don't suppose David is going to drive for Lanston in Atlanta, is he?"

"I don't think so," she answered.

"It ain't much," Arnie said, "but I've got another car. Some of these teams have fifteen, I only had two, but one of them's just sitting there in a barn at home. Ain't got a motor for it, though. Maybe David would want to drive it. Maybe his crew could brush the spider webs and pigeon droppings off of it and make it into a halfway decent piece."

"We can probably find out in a hurry," she said, and she dialed David's number on her cell phone. He answered and she told him Arnie Shale wanted to talk to him.

Arnie made the offer and Beth watched a grin spread across his face. He handed her the phone and said, "He's on his way."

DAVID LANDED HIS plane in Birmingham. Beth waited for him in the hangar, and a dozen people watched as he greeted her with an embrace and kiss that lasted so long that a couple of mechanics applauded.

When they reached her convertible Miata he said, "Let's put the top down."

"Don't you know it's winter, Dirt Dauber?" she asked. "But what the heck; we won't freeze."

Other motorists must have questioned their sanity as they drove along the interstate, unprotected from the cold November air. They drew more stares after they turned off the highway and moved through the quaint downtown of Springville, the hamlet in which Arnie Shale had lived his entire life.

"Nice village," David said.

"There's something to be said for a thin telephone book," Beth said.

"It would be a good place to raise children," David reckoned.

"Tall, dark, and handsome boys," Beth said.

"Or petite blonde girls," her passenger said.

They found Arnie Shale's house on a country road. It was an old but neat white frame structure shaded by a huge oak. His mother was sweeping the long front porch. She gazed at them until she recognized Beth, then she turned her back on them.

"Arnie's mother hates racing," Beth said. "He said to come around to the barn in back."

The barn's double doors were spread open and Arnie was sitting in his wheelchair, parked beside the *St. Clair County Special*. "Welcome, welcome," he greeted them. "Sorry I can't get up."

David thanked Arnie for the use of the car and Beth kissed the boy on the cheek. Then David began inspecting the Ford racer.

"What's this?" he asked, pointing to something on the hood.

"Fish bones," Arnie said. "We had a fish fry and used the car for the table. We forgot to clean the little bones off, and now they're glued to the hood."

David laughed heartily. "Pappy Draper is a miracle worker," he said, "but I'll bet he's never been faced with removing fish bones from a race car."

"Is your crew coming?" Arnie asked. "I heard Lanston fired them, so I didn't know. I was going to say my volunteers would help, if they weren't."

"I called Pappy, and he talked to the guys, and they want to beat Lanston and Vern Parchman as bad as I do. They'll be arriving from Charlotte pretty soon. They can whip this car into fine shape.

"There's one problem," David continued. "We don't have an engine. It will be difficult to find one just before the last race of the season— one that's capable of winning, I mean. I phoned a couple of engine builders and they didn't have anything. Some others might have some sub-par motors they'd dump on me just to get rid of them, but that wouldn't help us."

Arnie made coffee and they waited. He showed them his cow and his horse and his pigs and his chickens. "Lots of catfish in there," he said, pointing to a little pond in the pasture, and he was delighted when David suggested they try to catch them. Arnie fetched three rods and a tomato can full of worms from the barn, and they sat on the bank and fished.

Beth wondered how David could be so calm, so relaxed, so joyous, when Herman Lanston was attempting to cheat him out of the championship. She asked him.

"Sometimes it's good to escape your own little world for awhile," he said. "It's good to remember there are other things under the sun than whatever's driving you nuts. Fishing in a farm pond in Alabama isn't a bad way to spend your time. Even if the fish aren't biting."

Beth snuggled her head onto his shoulder and they didn't speak for ten minutes. The fish didn't open their mouths, either. The ringing of David's cell phone shattered their reverie. "Hello," he said. "Who? Brad Statham? Well, as a matter of fact, Brad, I'm fishing in Arnie Shale's catfish pond with Arnie and Beth Barrett, the racing writer of *The Birmingham News*."

David listened intently for several minutes, then said, "Brad, I'm speechless. I hope someday I can do something this wonderful for you. Thanks, and goodbye."

David gazed at the pond and shook his head in amazement. Beth thought she saw the hint of a tear in the corner of his eye. "Brad Statham is sending us a crackerjack motor," he said. "He caught Pappy before the crew left Charlotte, and Pappy is bringing it."

"Why?" Beth asked.

"As you know, Brad passed Parchman on the last lap and finished third in the last race. It was his best finish of the season.

"His sponsor doesn't have a lot of money to spend on racing, but the company had done well over the last couple of months or so, and his sponsor bought him two great engines. He used one at Homestead, and he was going to use the other one at Atlanta.

"But one of my crewmen told one of his crewmen about our problem, and Brad wants me to have the motor instead. He despises Herman Lanston for the way Lanston treated him when Brad was his driver, and he wants me to win the championship. He said it's important that the bad guys don't always win. Somewhere along the way, Herman backstabbed Brad's sponsor, too, so the sponsor was all for letting me have the motor. Brad will use the same one he had at Homestead, with four hundred miles on it.

"Brad needs a victory, and he might have won Atlanta with the motor he's giving me. I'm touched, Beth. First Arnie and now Brad—they've come to my rescue.

"Also, Brad said you interviewed him once and he asked you not to write anything that would have him criticizing Lanston, because he was afraid of what Lanston might do. He said for me to tell you that was beneath him, and he hopes you will write a story about him giving me the motor in hopes we can beat Parchman and Lanston for the championship."

"You'd better believe I will," she said.

DAVID'S MECHANICS arrived in an armada of pickup trucks, vans, and cars. David and Arnie and Beth greeted them at the entrance to the barn. Pappy made for Beth and gave her a big kiss on the cheek. "I'm working for free," he told David, "so you can't do nothing about me kissing your girl."

"I guess you're right," David said, embracing his crew chief and patting him on the back.

Pappy said he and the mechanics would sleep in the barn and in their vans for the duration. They brought blankets and sleeping bags. "It'll take several days to whip this thing into shape, but we can do it. I ain't even touched the car yet, and I've already spotted something I can do to make her handle better."

Beth took a notebook and pen from her purse. "I do have to make a living," she said. "I've got a story to write. Tell me, Mr. Marlow, what you're doing in Springville, Alabama, of all places."

She interviewed David and Pappy and Arnie, and then she kissed David goodbye, told him to sleep well in the barn, and drove back to her warm apartment—where she wrote a story that answered the question of whether David Marlow would drive for Herman Lanston at Atlanta, that outlined the plan for him to drive Arnie Shale's *St. Clair County Special*, powered by Brad Statham's engine, in the showdown for the championship.

It was an exclusive story and the editors liked it so much they decreed it wouldn't run in the sports section, but across the top of the front page of *The Birmingham News*.

DAVID DIDN'T HAVE the luxury of a qualifying engine for the final race of the season, a power plant designed to provide a massive burst of speed for a couple of laps. But he viewed that as a minor inconvenience. He used his race engine in time trials and won the thirty-second starting position in the forty-three-car lineup. Vern Parchman won the pole position.

After Beth's story on the Marlow-Shale-Statham triumvirate ran, reporters had flocked to Arnie's barn for interviews. Each of them asked the same question: Why wouldn't Marlow drive for Lanston? He answered each of them with, "No comment."

Reporters who interviewed Lanston told David he was furious because David wouldn't drive a second Lanston Farms car, that he declared David was under contract to do so, and Lanston might sue him, that David's refusal was a reflection on Lanston's integrity, and Lanston had always been a man of integrity. They asked David to comment on that development.

"No comment," he said.

They continued to quiz David at the speedway in Atlanta but he smiled and said, "No comment," and finally the exasperated reporters gave up.

Chapter 18

*F*ew stock car races had ever generated as much interest as this
one had. The story line had everything. The leaders were tied
atop the points standings. David had refused to drive Lanston's car,
instead accepting the offer of a car owned by an Alabama country boy.
It would be powered by an engine given to David by a former Lanston
driver. Veteran star Vern Parchman was driving in his final race before
retirement.

The weather cooperated. Race day was chilly but not oppressively
cold. The skies over Atlanta Motor Speedway were clear.

Beth chose to cover the event from the infield press room. She could
easily rush to the garage and interview any driver who fell out of the
race. She would have to rely on television to keep up with the action.
(Most reporters wouldn't admit it, but watching a race on TV was the
best way to stay apprised.)

Beth walked with David as he headed for the *St. Clair County Special*,
which waited on pit road. He reached for her hand and held it as
bystanders wished him luck and checked out his girlfriend. Beth smiled
when she heard an old man say, "She's a cutie, all right."

They kissed at the entrance to pit road, her stopping point. "I love
you," David said.

"I love you," Beth said.

She watched through the fence as he strolled to his pit, spoke a few words to Pappy Draper, and contorted himself into the car.

Arnie Shale and his wheelchair were in David's pit. He wanted to experience the sights and sounds and smells of the race. Herman Lanston walked by, and Beth saw him glare at Arnie. Arnie just grinned.

The grand marshal was an actor who had starred in a racing movie, so he delivered the traditional command with a dramatic intonation appropriate to the occasion:

"Gentlemen, start your engines!"

Beth stood behind the pits and watched the first five laps. Already Parchman, the pole sitter, had fallen back to tenth place. With another driver, that could have meant his car wasn't as strong as it had qualified. Beth knew that in Parchman's case it probably meant his car was so strong that he could afford to coast and let the hot dogs fight it out at the front.

She returned to the infield press room and settled in for a long afternoon. The TV announcer pointed out that David Marlow had slipped from thirty-second place to thirty-fifth. She knew he wasn't sandbagging, though. "Go, Dirt Dauber," she whispered.

"Sports writers are supposed to be neutral," a reporter from a Los Angeles paper kidded her.

"Was it that obvious?" Beth asked.

"Yep."

Beth knew that the mechanical skills of Pappy and his crewmen had not been enough to put the *St. Clair County Special* into a comfortable handling mode. It lacked the refinements of a car crafted by a major team. But David had to make do with what was available, and in this case it was a strange-looking racer covered with signatures of Arnie's well-wishers.

She knew he would extract from the car everything that was in it—but would that be enough?

Raider Slater wasn't bashful. His car was running and handling perfectly, and he put it in the lead and kept it there.

David, meanwhile, languished near the rear of the field. "It's pushing something awful," he told Pappy over the radio. "I have some ideas about adjustments that might help. But we'll have to have a caution flag to make them, because they'll take a minute or so."

One doesn't have to have mechanical knowledge to cover racing any more than one has to know how footballs are manufactured to cover football. Beth had no clue what David was talking about as he rattled off a list of technical instructions to Pappy.

But no caution flag waved. David's car ran as if it were stuck in mud. He was in forty-second place in the forty-three-car field.

"At this rate, we're going to get lapped before the first pit stop," David said. "Slater's got it hooked up, hasn't he?"

"That he has," Pappy said.

Beth switched to Parchman's channel in time to hear Herman Lanston tell his driver, "Marlow's running like a snail in that junker. You can lap him. I want to see you put him a lap down. Go to it!"

"Herman, I'm as comfortable as if I was at home on my den sofa watching Andy Griffith," Parchman said. "I'll have to really push it to take the lead from Slater, much less lap Marlow."

"I said lap him and I mean lap him!" Lanston screamed.

"Okay, okay."

Parchman went high and Parchman went low, passing car after car. He reached Slater's bumper, but Slater shut the door when he tried to drive inside him.

"Damn!" Lanston screamed. "There's a caution flag!"

A couple of mid-field drivers tangled and spun out, and the yellow waved. Slater held the lead over Parchman. One by one the cars pitted, until the track itself was almost empty.

Pappy and his crew swarmed over the *St. Clair County Special*, making the adjustments David had ordered. They weren't finished, but

David had to speed back onto the track for a single lap to keep the pace car from putting him a lap down. Then he darted back into the pits and his mechanics resumed their work.

Finally, Pappy banged on the hood, a signal for him to return to the track. He did, at the rear of the field, but saved from being lapped.

The green flag was displayed, and Parchman backed out of his duel with Slater. Since the prospect of embarrassing Marlow by lapping him had disappeared, he resumed his deliberate tactics.

Beth was frustrated because the TV commentators didn't mention David. She left the press center, spotted some celebrants atop an old school bus in the infield, and asked if she might join them. She would try to follow David's progress—or lack of same—that from that perch.

"Come on up, hon," a shirtless fan invited. "Got a beer and a chicken leg just for you."

Beth climbed the steel ladder that was attached to the side of the bus, a rough and ready vehicle that had been painted crimson and adorned with three-foot-tall white letters: *Roll Tide*.

"Who you for?" the good ole boy asked.

"David Marlow," she said. "Who are you for?"

"Raider Slater," he said cordially, "but we'll share our beer and fried chicken with you anyway. Maybe we can convert you."

He and his five friends introduced themselves. They seemed harmless, and when she accepted a chicken leg and turned down a beer, one of them yelped, "Good idea, hon. That old demon rum will make your pretty yeller hair fall out. Look what it did to me." He rubbed his bald head, and his buddies thought that was the funniest thing they had ever seen.

She watched as David advanced into the top fifteen. But then a couple of cars passed his. He had improved the handling of the *St. Clair County Special*, but he hadn't cured it.

Beth listened on the scanner. "I've got some more ideas," David told Pappy, "but we'll have to have another caution flag." Again he instructed the crew chief on the changes he wanted made.

"Been meaning to get me one of them scanners," one of the good ole boys said. "Mind if I listen to Slater and his crew for a second?"

"Only if you give me another chicken leg," Beth said, and he whooped and hollered and called her a good ole girl and fetched another drumstick. Beth tuned in Slater's channel and handed the scanner to the fan.

He furrowed his brow for a minute, and then he let out a yell, raising his arms to the sky and almost letting the scanner shoot through his chicken-greasy hands. "Raider just told them he can't lose this race! Said he's got the best car he's ever had, and he's got the race in the bag. I got to get me one of these things."

Beth ate a second drumstick, wished the guys a nice day, and descended the ladder. They told her they were sorry they hadn't converted her into a Slater fan, but they hoped Marlow would be the runner-up, second only to their man, Raider.

As she opened the door of the infield press center she heard the TV announcer declare that a second yellow flag was waving. David could pit and get his adjustments during the slow-motion caution period.

When the race resumed under green, Marlow challenged Parchman for ninth place. David couldn't pass him, but Vern was forced to step up the pace, and soon they were running third and fourth.

"The motor's great," David told Draper. "The handling is much better, but I still can't hold it between the ditches well enough to get by Parchman. We'll try something else during the next caution."

Beth thought about the nature of racing. Teams base strategy on eventual crashes by the opposition. It would be like a basketball team drawing up plays based on the opposing point guard's eventually pulling a muscle. Occasionally there were races without a caution, but they were few and far between.

Again the yellow waved, and again the cars pitted, and again Draper made the adjustments Marlow had asked for.

But this time David had guessed wrong. His car retreated to the middle of the pack. "It didn't work," he told Draper. "We're in trouble."

They were silent for many laps and Beth knew David was calling on his years of mechanical and driving experience, searching for an answer to the problem. Meanwhile, cars shot by him.

And Parchman rode in second place, on Slater's bumper. Raider had earned five bonus points for leading a lap, and so had Parchman, who had been in front under caution when Slater had pitted first. Slater was well on his way to picking up five bonus points for leading the most laps, too. Marlow hadn't even threatened to take the lead.

"It's too early to tell, of course," said a TV commentator, "but my guess is that Slater is going to win this race and Parchman is going to win the championship. Parchman and Marlow entered the day tied in the standings, twenty-one points ahead of Slater. Even if Slater wins the race and leads the most laps, Parchman can still win the championship by finishing fourth today. Marlow seems to be out of the picture. The injured Arnie Shale's letting him drive his *St. Clair County Special*, the odd-looking car with all the signatures on it, made for a wonderful story, but it's apparent it isn't a car that's up to taking David to Victory Lane or to the season's throne room."

"I agree totally with your assessment," his color man said.

Beth sighed. The thought of Herman Lanston stealing the championship gave her the same helpless feeling she had experienced as a grammar school girl when a car had run over her puppy and the driver had sped away.

"There's a spinout in turn one, and the starter is waving the caution flag," the TV commentator said.

Beth tuned in David's channel and heard him say, "I think I've figured it out, Pappy! I know what's making this car so hardheaded." Again he rattled off arcane instructions to the crew chief.

"I know one thing," David said as he returned to the track after his mechanics had made the adjustments, "if I guessed wrong we can forget the championship, because we're running out of time."

Again the time required for the changes had plummeted him to the back of the field. There were many carnival-colored, speeding obstacles between David Marlow and the lead.

But, under green, he picked them off, one by one. He was thirtieth, then twentieth, then fifteenth. "Maybe we are wrong about Marlow," the TV commentator said. "Whatever elixir his crew gave the car on that last pit stop, it seems to have rejuvenated the *St. Clair County Special.*"

Then David was tenth. Then fifth. Then he was third on the rear bumper of Vern Parchman, who was on Raider Slater's rear bumper. "We definitely were wrong about Marlow," the TV commentator said.

Even if there weren't a caution period, everyone would have to pit one more time. Beth was glad she wasn't one of David's crewmen. Theirs was an awesome responsibility. The race and the championship could hinge on an extraneous move by a tire changer or the fuel man. A second lost in the pits could be decisive.

A greasy young man tapped Beth on the shoulder. She recognized him as one of Marlow's mechanics. "David wants you in the pits for his last stop," he said. "Here's a crew pass."

She took the credential, but before she could ask for an explanation, he was out the door of the press room and headed for the pits.

She showed the pass to a security guard and walked beyond the fence that separated the pits from the rest of the world. She stood behind the wall at David's pit and called Pappy's name. He wore earphones, though, and he couldn't hear her.

A crewman lifted Pappy's earphone and said something to him. The crew chief turned and saw Beth. She shrugged and opened her palms toward the sky, signs she was bewildered by David's summons.

"I have no idea," Draper yelled against the roar of the cars. "All I know is that David said he wanted you here for our final pit stop."

Five minutes later Marlow made that final stop. Slater and Parchman pitted on the same lap.

David lowered the netting of the driver's window and shouted, "Will you marry me, Beth?"

She was speechless. But only for a moment. "Yes, I will, David."

Then the window netting was up and he was away, still trailing Parchman, who was still trailing Slater. Eight laps remained.

Beth listened to her scanner. "Tell her I wanted that bit of inspiration to propel me around these two guys," David told Pappy. The crew chief glanced at her, and she gave him the thumbs-up sign, indicating that she had heard.

Pappy and his men had simply changed all four tires and administered a splash of fuel. They made no further adjustments. That told Beth the car was right for the showdown.

The trio ran in that order for four laps. Beth tuned in Slater's channel and heard his crew chief saying, "Stay calm, Raider, stay calm. Just stay calm, now."

What could that mean except that the young driver wasn't staying calm?

He drove into the third turn too hard, his racer bobbled, and Parchman shot by him on the inside. Slater over-corrected, and Marlow had to back off to keep from driving up onto Raider's trunk lid.

Meanwhile, Parchman extended his lead.

"You've got it, Vern! You've got it!" Herman Lanston screamed into the radio. "You've got the race and the championship!"

The savvy that comes from a combination of being good at what you do and from having done it for a long time told David to not give Slater time to recover his calm, to prevent his analyzing the situation. When they were square on the front straightaway, and he was sure he wouldn't spin Slater out, David rammed the rear of Raider's car.

It was a maneuver intended to unnerve and confuse the younger driver, and it worked. Slater darted down to protect the inside lane as they entered the first turn. Again he drove in too hard, his car bobbled, and Marlow passed him on the outside.

David trailed Parchman by fifty yards with three laps to go.

"How 'bout it?" Pappy asked.

"Arnie's car is handling like a gem and Brad's motor is stronger than a platter of garlic," David answered. "Now, if your driver can just do his part. Man, I wish we had four more laps instead of three, though."

Beth watched on television as David drove what a TV color man, who was a former racing champion himself, called "as perfect a line around this place as there is."

He caught Parchman as they came out of the second turn on the last lap.

"Catching him's one thing, passing him's another," the TV commentator said.

Beth froze as she heard Herman Lanston's instructions to Parchman: "I don't care if you have to knock his car into the grandstand, you'd better not let him pass you."

"Go to hell, Herman," said Parchman. "I'm not going to wreck him to win the race or the championship."

Marlow followed Parchman through the third and fourth turns, the leader protecting the shorter inside line in textbook fashion. David had no choice but to try him on the outside as they sped down the frontstretch to the checkered flag.

He mustn't drive too wide or the extra distance would exact an insurmountable penalty. He pulled alongside Parchman's racer, and the TV commentator said, "I don't believe you could get a sheet of paper between those two cars."

Certainly at the flashpoint you couldn't have inserted a sheet of paper between them—for they slammed sides.

David's racer went into a barrel roll. Parchman's remained upright but it slid sideways.

They crossed the finish line in those attitudes.

Beth knew David had won the race and the championship, because his car had reached the line first. But she didn't care about trophies and titles. She just wanted David's car to stop rolling—but on it went, over and over and over.

She ran to the pit gate, flashed her crew pass, and scurried behind Pappy and his mechanics as they hustled toward David's racer, which finally stopped upside down, a mangled, smoking thing that didn't resemble a car.

She felt a hand on her shoulder. It was Vern Parchman's. He had exited his car and rushed to his fallen opponent.

Firemen stood poised with their extinguishers, and members of the rescue team cut away the netting of the driver's window.

A helmet rolled out of the window and onto the racing surface, and Beth grabbed Parchman's arm.

But then she heard a familiar voice: "I'm okay," David said. "Back off and let me out of this thing."

He crawled from the wreckage, and Beth ran past safety personnel before they could restrain her. She and David embraced and kissed on national television. Thousands of fans in the grandstand clapped and whistled and cheered.

David spotted Parchman and said, "Some finish, huh, Vern?"

"I think they'll remember that one for a while," Parchman said. Then he added, "David, I raced you clean and you raced me clean. That's the only way to do it. It was just a racing accident, nobody's fault."

"Exactly," David said.

The new champion of stock car racing had one arm around his fiancée's shoulder and one arm around his crew chief's waist. "They'll have to sweep up what's left of Arnie's car in a dustpan," David told Pappy, "but I'll use some of the championship bonus to buy him two brand new ones to start next season."

David whispered into Beth's ear, "After I do the post-race press conference and you write your story, let's get in my plane and head to Daytona Beach. Then we'll get married at the courthouse first thing in the morning."

She pictured her mother in all her matronly glory at her daughter's majestic church wedding and at the magnificent country club reception afterward.

Nah. A courthouse wedding was more appealing to the betrothed.

"Sounds like a heck of a plan to me, Champ," Beth said.

About the Author

Clyde Bolton is the author of sixteen books, including six novels and ten works of nonfiction. In 2001 he retired after forty-six years in the newspaper business to devote full time to writing books. He was a sports writer for *The Birmingham News* for forty years, and for twenty-eight of those years he was that paper's auto racing beat writer, so he brings special insight to the pages of *Turn Left on Green*.

In 1985 he won the American Motorsports Award of Excellence for the best newspaper story in the nation on Winston Cup Racing. The All-American Football Foundation honored him in 1996 with its Lifetime Achievement in Sports Writing Award. Three times he was voted Alabama's Sports Writer of the Year and three times he was its Sports Columnist of the Year. In 2001 Bolton was inducted into the Alabama Sports Writers Hall of Fame. In addition to *The Birmingham News*, Bolton worked for *The Anniston Star*, *The Gadsden Times*, and *The Montgomery Advertiser* in Alabama, and *The LaGrange Daily News* in Georgia.

He and his wife, Sandra, the parents of three adult sons, live in Trussville, Alabama.

Bolton's nonfiction books are *The Crimson Tide*, *War Eagle*, *Unforgettable Days in Southern Football*, *Bolton's Best Stories of Auto Racing*, *The Basketball Tide*, *They Wore Crimson*, *Silver Britches*, *Talladega Superspeedway*, *Remembering Davey*, and *The Alabama Gang*. His novels are *Water Oaks*, *Ivy*, *And Now I See*, *The Lost Sunshine*, *Nancy Swimmer*, and *Turn Left on Green*.

197